The Pilgrim's Progress

The Pilgrim's Progress

John Bunyan

BARBOUR
PUBLISHING

Cover image © Yolande De Kort/Trevillion Images

Published by Barbour Publishing, Inc., P.O. Box 719, Uhrichsville, Ohio 44683, www.barbourbooks.com.

Our mission is to publish and distribute inspirational products offering exceptional value and biblical encouragement to the masses.

Member of the
Evangelical Christian
Publishers Association

Printed in the United States of America.

The Pilgrim's Progress has been printed, read, and translated more often than any book other than the Bible. People of all ages have found delight in the simple, earnest story of Christian, the Pilgrim. The events seem lifelike, following each other rapidly and consistently.

John Bunyan was born in 1628 in the village of Elstow, England. His father was a tinker, a lowly occupation. Nevertheless, his father sent him to school to learn to read and write.

In 1674 Bunyan married an orphan who was a praying Christian. She led her husband to the Lord, and he was baptized. Bunyan soon began to preach but was arrested and thrown into prison for preaching without receiving permission from the established church. He remained there for twelve years, during which time he wrote this book.

Reading *The Pilgrim's Progress* is not only a pleasurable experience, but a life-changing one as well.

A man clothed in rags and weighed down by a great burden on his back stood facing away from his own house. He opened the Bible he held in his hand, and as he read, he wept and trembled. Finally, no longer able to contain himself, he cried, "What shall I do?"

In this plight he entered his home and spoke his mind. "Oh, dear wife and children, I am distressed by this burden upon my back. Moreover, I am certain our city will be burned by fire from heaven. We shall all perish unless I find a way for us to escape."

His family was amazed—not because they thought what he said was true, but because they thought he was out of his head. They thought sleep might calm him down, so they got him to bed. But nighttime was as troubling to him as the day, and he spent the night in sighs and tears.

In the morning he declared he was worse than the night before. He spoke to them again, but they didn't want to hear him. Since sleep hadn't helped, they decided to treat his craziness by mocking, scolding, and ignoring him.

He withdrew, often alone in the fields, to pray for them and read his Bible. For some days he spent his time this way.

One day he stood in the fields and cried, "What must I do to be saved?" He looked this way and that way as if he would run, but knew not where.

A man approached. "I am Evangelist. Why are you crying so?"

The man answered, "Sir, I read in this Bible that I am condemned to die, and after that to come to judgment. I find that I am not willing to do the first, nor able to do the second."

Evangelist asked, "Why are you not willing to die, since this life is so full of evil?"

The man answered, "I fear that this burden on my back will sink me to hell. I am not ready to go to judgment. And my thoughts make me despair."

"Why then are you standing still?"

"I don't know where to go!"

"Read this." Evangelist gave him a roll of parchment that said, "Fly from the wrath to come."

The man asked, "Where should I fly?"

Evangelist pointed beyond a wide plain. "Do you see the distant wicket gate?"

"No."

"Do you see the distant shining light?"

"I think I do."

Then Evangelist said, "Follow the light and it will bring you to the gate. When you knock, the gatekeeper will tell you what to do from there."

So the man began to run. Seeing him, his wife and children cried after him to return. But the man put his fingers in his ears and ran on, crying, "Life! Life! Eternal life!"

The neighbors also came out to see him run, and some mocked, others threatened, and some cried after him to return. Two neighbors, Obstinate and Pliable, followed him and overtook him, attempting to persuade him to return with them.

He answered, "You dwell in the City of Destruction. And dying there, you will sink into a place that burns with fire and brimstone. Come along with me."

"What!" said Obstinate. "And leave friends and comforts behind?"

"Yes," answered Christian, for that was now the man's name. "Those are not worthy to be compared with what I seek. I seek an inheritance incorruptible, undefiled, that never fades away. It awaits in heaven, to be bestowed on those who diligently seek it. Read about it in my Bible."

"Phooey on your Bible," said Obstinate. "Will you go back with us or not?"

"No, because I have 'put my hand to the plow.'"

"Come, neighbor Pliable," said Obstinate, "he is a fool and wiser in his own eyes than seven men who can render a reason. Let us go home without him."

Pliable hesitated. "If what good Christian says is true, the things he looks for are better than ours. My heart longs to go with him."

"What? You are a fool, too. I will be no companion of such misled fantasies," said Obstinate and turned back. "Be wise and come back with me."

When Obstinate was gone, Christian and Pliable walked on across the plain.

"Are you certain the words of your book are true?" Pliable asked Christian.

"Yes, the Bible was made by He who cannot lie. There is an endless kingdom to inhabit, and everlasting life. We will be given crowns of glory and garments that will make us shine like the sun."

"These are pleasant thoughts," said Pliable. "What else does your Bible say?"

"There will be no more crying, no more sorrow. We shall be with seraphim, and cherubim, and creatures that will dazzle our eyes. We shall meet with tens of thousands who have gone before us, loving and holy, everyone walking in the sight of God—all well again, and clothed in the garment of immortality."

"But how can we share in that?"

"The Lord has recorded in this Bible," answered Christian, "that if we are willing to have it, He will bestow it on us freely."

"The hearing of this is enough to delight one's heart. Come, let us quicken our pace."

But Christian answered, "I cannot go as fast as I would like because of the burden that is on my back."

Because they were careless, however, they became mired in a bog in the midst of the plain called the Slough of Despond.

Pliable, angry now, cried out to Christian, "Is this the happiness and pleasure you told me about? If the journey starts out this way, what will the rest be like? If I get out of here alive, you can take your journey without me."

He pulled himself out on the side nearest his home, and he lost no time putting Christian behind him.

Christian struggled across the Slough of Despond toward the wicket gate, but he could not get out because of the burden on his back. A man approached from the other side.

"What are you doing here?" the man asked.

"I'm on my way to the gate that I may escape the wrath to come. But I fell into this slough instead."

"Why didn't you look for the steps?" asked the man.

"Fear followed me so hard, I fell in the Slough."

"I am Help." And Help plucked Christian out and bid him on his way, explaining, "The Slough of Despond cannot be mended so that travelers pass safely. It is the accumulation of scum and filth that continually runs from the conviction for sin. Because even though the sinner is awakened to his lost condition, fears and doubts and discouraging apprehensions still run from his soul and settle in the Slough. It is not the pleasure of the King that the Slough remain so bad. There are, by direction of the Lawgiver, certain good and substantial steps, placed evenly through the very midst of the Slough. Yet because of the filth the steps are hardly seen, or if they are, dizzy men fall by the side anyway."

Now Christian, walking across the plain by himself, met Mr. Worldly Wiseman, who dwelt in Carnal Policy, a very great town close to the City of Destruction. Worldly Wiseman had some inkling of Christian, because Christian's departure was already gossip in other places.

Worldly Wiseman greeted Christian and

asked where he was going.

"To the wicket gate across the plain," Christian replied. "I've been told that is the entrance to the way to get rid of this heavy burden."

"Will you heed my counsel?" asked Worldly Wiseman.

"If it is good, I will."

"There is no more dangerous and troublesome way in the world than that which Evangelist has directed you. Hear me; you will meet weariness, pain, hunger, peril, sword, lions, dragons, darkness, and, in a word, death."

"But this burden on my back is more terrible to me. I don't care what I meet if I also meet deliverance from my burden."

"How did you get that burden?"

"By reading this Bible."

"I thought so. It has happened to other weak men, too. Remedy is at hand. But instead of the dangers, you will meet with safety, friendship, and content."

"Show me this secret of yours."

"In the next village of Morality, there is a gentleman whose name is Legality. He has the skill to help you rid yourself of your burden. His house is less than a mile away. If he is not at home, his son, Civility, can take care of you as well as his father would. Once you are healed, you can send for your wife and children to join you there, as there are houses standing empty and the cost of living is very reasonable."

Christian, eager to be rid of his burden, thought the advice was sound. "Sir, which is the way to this honest man's house?"

"You must go to that mountain over there. The first house is his."

So Christian went out of his way to go to Legality's house. The burden seemed even heavier, and the mountain soon loomed over the path and burst flashes of fire. Christian quaked with fear and began to be sorry he'd taken Worldly Wiseman's counsel. At that moment he saw Evangelist walking toward him and he blushed for shame.

"What are you doing here, Christian?" asked Evangelist.

Christian stood speechless before him.

"Are you not the man I spoke to outside the walls of the City of Destruction?"

"Yes, sir."

"How do you come to be here? This is out of the way I showed you."

"A gentleman showed me a better way, short and not so rife with difficulties as the one you sent me on. But when I came to this place and saw the danger of going forward, I stopped for fear. Now I don't know what to do."

Evangelist then spoke. "God said, 'My righteous one will live by faith. And if he shrinks back,

I will not be pleased with him.' You have begun to reject the counsel of the Most High. You drew back your foot from the way of peace."

Christian fell down. "Woe is me, for I am undone!"

Evangelist took his right hand. "The Lord says, 'Every sin and blasphemy will be forgiven.' So be not faithless, but believing."

Christian stood up, revived a little.

Evangelist went on, "Worldly Wiseman, who savors only the doctrine of this world, did three terrible things. First, he turned you from the way. Secondly, Worldly Wiseman disparaged the Cross to you. Thirdly, he sent you on the way to death."

Evangelist went on to explain how Worldly Wiseman almost beguiled Christian out of his salvation. The mountain looming over them was Mount Sinai. Then Evangelist called out to the heavens for confirmation.

In bursts of fire, words rumbled from the mountain: "All who rely on observing the law are under a curse, for it is written: 'Cursed is everyone who does not continue to do everything written in the Book of the Law.'"

"And no one is able to obey every law," explained Evangelist.

Christian now called himself a thousand fools for listening to Worldly Wiseman's advice.

Thinking there was no hope for him now but death, he asked Evangelist, "Is it possible for me to go back to the wicket gate? Or am I abandoned and sent back in shame? Is my sin too great to be forgiven?"

"Your sin, indeed, is great," Evangelist said. "But it is forgiven. The man at the gate will receive you, for he has goodwill for men. But take heed that you do not turn aside from the way again, or you might perish."

When Evangelist had bid him Godspeed, Christian hurried back, refusing to speak to anyone, and found the way again. In time he found the wicket gate. Over the small narrow gate was written: KNOCK, AND THE DOOR WILL BE OPENED TO YOU.

He knocked, saying: "May I now enter here? Will he within open to sorry me, though I have been an undeserving rebel? Then shall I not fail to sing his lasting praise on high."

At last a serious man came to the gate. "I am Goodwill. Who knocks? From where have you come? What do you want?"

"I am a poor, burdened sinner. I come from the City of Destruction, but I am going to Celestial City, so that I might be delivered from the wrath to come. I am told this gate is the way. Are you willing to let me in?"

"With all my heart." Goodwill opened the

narrow gate and yanked Christian inside.

"Why did you do that?" sputtered Christian.

"There is a strong castle near here where the devil Beelzebub is the captain. He and his army shoot arrows at those who come to this gate, in the hope they die before they enter."

"Thank you for your quick action," Christian praised Goodwill.

"Who directed you here?"

"Evangelist. He told me you would tell me what to do."

"Why do you come alone? Did no one know of your coming?"

"Yes, my wife and children saw me first and called after me to return. Then some of my neighbors joined their cry. But I refused to listen and came on my way. Still I allowed myself to stray from the path. It amazes me that I am allowed to enter now."

"We turn no one away, no matter what they have done before they come to us," Goodwill assured him. Then Goodwill beckoned Christian to follow him. "I will teach you about the way you must go. Look before you. Do you see the narrow way? That is the way you must go. It was laid out by the patriarchs, prophets, Christ, and His apostles. It is as straight as a rule can make it."

"But are there no turnings and windings by which a stranger might lose his way?"

"There are many ways that are crooked and wide, but only the right way is straight and narrow."

Then Christian asked, "Would you help me remove the burden upon my back? I have tried to do it myself, but I cannot do it without help."

"Be content to bear it until you come to the place of deliverance. There it will fall from your back of itself."

As Christian prepared to continue his journey, Goodwill told him, "When you have gone some distance, you will come to Interpreter's home. He will show you many things that will help you on your journey."

Christian went on until he came to a house. He knocked and called out, "I am going to the Celestial City. I was told at the gate that if I called here, the Interpreter would show me excellent things."

The door opened. A man said, "I am the Interpreter. Come in."

His servant lit a candle and Christian followed the Interpreter through the house to a private room where a portrait hung on the wall. The very somber man in the picture had his eyes lifted to heaven, the Best of Books in his hand, and the Law of Truth written on his lips. The world was behind his back and a crown of gold hung over his head. The man seemed to plead with men.

"What does this mean?" asked Christian.

"This man's work is to know and unfold the darkness to sinners. He has put the world behind him for the love he has for his Master's service. I have shown you this picture first because this man is the only guide authorized by the Lord of the place where you are going. Take good heed. In your journey you will meet with some who pretend to lead you the right way, but their way leads to death."

Then Interpreter took Christian by the hand and led him into a very large parlor that was full of dust. He called for a man to sweep, who went about his job so vigorously Christian began to choke on the dust. Then Interpreter called a girl to bring water and sprinkle the room. When she finished, the room was swept and cleaned with pleasure.

"And what is the meaning of this?" asked Christian.

"This parlor is the heart of a man never sanctified by the grace of the Gospel. The dust is original sin and a lifetime of corruptions that pollute the man. The man who swept is the Law. The maiden who sprinkled water is the Gospel. Instead of cleansing the heart by its working, the Law increased sin in the heart, for it does not give power to subdue it. The Gospel vanquished sin, and the heart is made clean, fit for the King of Glory to enter."

The Interpreter took Christian into another room where two children sat in chairs. The older child, Passion, was restless. The younger child, Patience, sat quietly.

Christian asked, "What is the reason for Passion's discontent?"

The Interpreter said they had been told to wait one year for their reward. But Passion wanted it all now, while Patience was willing to wait. Then someone brought Passion a bag of treasure, which caused him to rejoice and scorn Patience. But he squandered the treasure, and it became rags.

"Explain this to me," said Christian.

"Passion is a figure for the men of this world who want everything now. Patience is a figure for the men who await that world which is yet to come. For men like Passion, they believe in the proverb, 'A bird in the hand is worth two in the bush.' "

"I see that Patience has the better wisdom because he waits for the best things, and in the world to come he will have much when Passion will only have rags."

"And there is one more benefit," Interpreter added. "The rewards of the next world never wear out, while the joys of this world don't last. For first must give place to last, but last gives place to nothing, for there is not another to follow."

"I see now that it is best to wait for things to come."

"This is truth. 'For what is seen is temporary, but what is unseen is eternal.'"

Then the Interpreter took Christian into a room where a fire was burning on one wall. A fiend stood by, constantly casting water on it. Yet the fire burned ever higher and hotter.

"What does this mean?" asked Christian.

"The fire is the work of grace wrought in your heart. The man trying to extinguish the fire is the devil. Come with me."

The Interpreter led him to the other side of the wall. A figure hidden from the other room constantly cast oil from a flask into the fire.

"What does this mean?" asked Christian.

"This is Christ, who constantly maintains the fire already begun in your heart with the oil of His grace. It is hard for the tempter to see how the work of grace is maintained in the heart."

Then the Interpreter took Christian to a pleasant place with a beautiful, stately palace. Upon the upper balcony, several people, clothed in gold, walked.

"May we go in?" Christian asked.

The Interpreter led him toward the door of the palace. A large group of men stood around the door, wanting to go in but not having the courage to go farther. Off to the side a man sat at a table with a book and an inkwell, waiting to take the name of any who entered. In the doorway stood many armored men resolved to hurt any who attempted to enter the palace.

A bold man approached the man at the table and said, "Write down my name, sir."

With that the bold man drew his sword, donned a helmet, and fiercely fought his way through the armed men at the door. Finally he prevailed and entered the palace. Inside, a pleasant voice sang: "Come in, come in: Eternal glory you shall win." And the man was clothed in many fine garments.

"I know the meaning of that," said Christian. "Let me get on the way."

"No," said the Interpreter. "Not until I have shown you more."

He led Christian into a very dark room, where a man sat in an iron cage. The man's eyes were lowered, his hands folded together, and he sighed as if heartbroken. The Interpreter encouraged Christian to talk with the man.

"Who are you?" asked Christian.

"I am what I was not at one time."

"Then what were you?"

"I once was a successful professor, both in my own estimation and in the eyes of others. Once I thought I was on the path for the Celestial City, and had the joy of anticipation of my arrival there."

"What are you now?"

"I am a man of despair, locked in this iron cage."

"But how did you get into this condition?"

"I sinned against the light of the Word and the goodness of God. I have grieved the Spirit, and He is gone. I tempted the devil, and he is come to me. I provoked God to anger, and He has left me. I have so hardened my heart I cannot repent. Oh, eternity! Eternity!"

Then Christian turned to the Interpreter and asked, "Is there no hope for this man?"

"Ask him," said the Interpreter.

"There is no hope," the man in the iron cage said in answer to Christian's question.

"But the Son of the Blessed is compassionate and merciful."

"I have crucified Him afresh. I have despised His person and His righteousness, I have counted His Blood an unholy thing and have despised the Spirit of grace. Therefore all that remains for me is certain judgment."

"Why did you bring yourself into this condition?"

"For the lusts, pleasures, and profits of this world that brought me much delight. But now they bite me and gnaw at me like a burning worm."

Then the Interpreter said to Christian,

"Remember this man's misery and let it be an everlasting caution to you."

Christian said, "God, help me shun the cause of this man's misery. Is it not time for me to go?"

"Wait until I show you one thing more."

The Interpreter led Christian into another room. A man rose from a bed, trembling.

"Why does this man tremble in this way?" Christian asked the Interpreter, who bade the man to answer.

The man said, "I dreamed that the heavens above were black, and it thundered, and the lightning flashed. Suddenly a trumpet blasted. In flaming fire was a Man on a cloud, attended by thousands. A voice said, 'Arise, you dead. Come to judgment.' The rocks broke apart, the graves opened, and the dead that were buried there came to life. Some of them were very glad and looked upward, but some hid themselves under the mountains. Then the Man on the cloud opened a book and bid them all to draw near. But a fierce flame kept the people from drawing too near, so that the distance between was as the distance between the judge and the prisoners. A voice cried, 'Gather together the tares, the chaff, and the stubble. Cast them into the burning lake.' A bottomless pit opened, emitting smoke and hideous noises. 'Gather My wheat into the barn,' cried the voice. Many people were carried away up to the clouds. But I was left behind! I tried to hide myself, but I could not, for the Man that sat upon the cloud kept His eye on me. My sins came into my mind, and my conscience accused me on every side. Then I woke up. . . ."

"But what made you so afraid of the dream?" Christian asked.

"I thought the Day of Judgment was come, and that I was not ready for it. But what frightened me most was that the angels gathered up several others and left me behind. My conscience bothered me, and the Judge constantly watched me, showing indignation in His countenance."

"Have you considered these things?" the Interpreter asked Christian.

"Yes, and they put me in hope and fear."

"Remember them so they will keep you in the way you must go."

Then Christian prepared to continue his journey.

The Interpreter sent him on his way, saying, "The Comforter is always with you, good Christian, to guide you in the way that leads to the Celestial City."

So Christian went on his way, saying:

Here I have seen things rare and profitable,
Things pleasant, dreadful, things to make me
stable

In what I have begun to take in hand;
Then let me think on them, and understand
What it was they showed me, and let me be
Thankful, oh good Interpreter, to see."

∽

The way was fenced on either side by a wall called Salvation. Christian ran, but not without great difficulty because of the burden on his back. He came to a rise, and there stood a cross, and below it a sepulcher. Just as he came to the cross, the burden fell from his back and tumbled into the mouth of the sepulcher.

With a grateful heart, Christian said, "He has given me rest by His sorrow, and life by His death." Then he stood awhile to look and wonder that the sight of the cross had eased his burden so easily.

As he stood looking at the cross and weeping, three Shining Ones came to him. "Peace be with you," they said. And one added, "Your sins are forgiven." Another stripped him of his rags and clothed him in an embroidered coat and other rich garments. The third put a mark on his forehead and gave him a rolled certificate with a seal. "Look at it as you go," said the Shining One, "and present it at the Celestial Gate."

Christian gave three leaps for joy and went

on the way singing:

> *"How far I did come laden with my sin;*
> *Nothing could ease the grief that I was in,*
> *Until I came here: What a place is this!*
> *Can this be the beginning of my bliss?*
> *Is this where the burden falls from my back?*
> *Can this be where the ropes of bondage crack?*
> *Bless'd cross! Bless'd sepulcher! Blessed rather be*
> *The Man who there was put to shame for me!"*

∽

When he came to the bottom of the hill, he saw three men fast asleep a little way off the road. Their ankles were chained. Christian cried, "Wake up and flee. I will help you take off your leg irons. The devil prowls like 'a roaring lion.' You will surely become prey for his teeth."

"I see no danger," said the one called Simple.

"After a little more sleep," answered the man called Sloth.

"Every tub must stand on its own bottom," said the third, Presumption. "Leave us alone."

And the men fell asleep again.

Christian went on, troubled that the men had so little regard for his offer of help. Soon he saw two men come tumbling over the wall onto the narrow way. They hurried to catch up with Christian.

"Where did you come from?" Christian asked. "And where are you going?"

"We are Formalist and Hypocrisy," they said. "We were born in Vain-Glory, and we are going to the Celestial City to get praise."

"Why didn't you come in at the gate at the beginning of the way? Don't you know that it is written: 'The man who does not enter by the gate, but climbs in by some other way, is a thief and a robber'?"

They replied, "It's too far away. So our custom for more than a thousand years is to take a shortcut, as you saw."

"But won't it be counted a trespass against the Lord of the Celestial City? Did you not violate His revealed will?"

"Don't trouble yourself," Formalist and Hypocrisy said. "We have tradition on our side, and they had witnesses who could prove they had not strayed from the accepted."

"But will your tradition pass a trial at law?"

"Since the tradition is one of long standing, any impartial judge would now consider it legal. We are on the way, just as you are. So why is your condition any better than ours?"

"I walk by the rule of my Master. You walk by the rude working of your own devices. The Lord of the Way already considers you thieves. So I doubt you will be found true men at the end of the way. You came in by yourselves without His direction, and you shall go out by yourselves—without His mercy."

The two men didn't answer. For a time they went along silently.

"We keep the laws and ordinances as conscientiously as you do," Formalist and Hypocrisy said. "Therefore we don't see how you are different from us, except for your coat. But we understand that some of your neighbors gave it to you to hide the shame of your nakedness."

"But laws and ordinances will not save you, since you didn't come in by the door," Christian explained. "However, the Lord of Celestial City gave me my coat to cover my nakedness. I take it as a token of His kindness to me, for I had nothing but rags. You may not have noticed, but I have a mark on my forehead. One of my Lord's most intimate associates placed it there the day my burden fell off my shoulders. Moreover, they gave me this sealed roll to comfort me by reading it as I go on the way, and when I arrive at the Celestial City, I am to give it back at the gate as a token of my salvation. All these things you lack because you didn't come in at the gate."

The two looked at each other and laughed. As they continued on the way, Christian stayed in front of his two companions. All three continued on the way, with Christian in the front. He often refreshed himself reading in the roll.

Soon they came to a spring at the foot of the Hill of Difficulty. Christian drank from the spring and saw that the narrow way went straight up the hill.

Christian began to go up the hill, saying:

"This hill, though high, I do long to ascend;
To me the difficulty won't offend.
For I perceive the way to life lies here:
Come pluck up, heart, let's neither faint nor fear;
Better, though difficult, the right way to go,
Than wrong, though easy, where the end is woe."

Two other paths went around the base of the hill. Supposing that it would lead them back to the path Christian was on, one of the two men following Christian took the path called Destruction. It led him into a wide field full of dark mountains where he stumbled and fell and rose no more. The other took the path called Danger, which led him into a great wood.

As Christian ascended, he fell to clamber on his hands and knees because of the steepness. About halfway up was a pleasant arbor made by the Lord of the Hill for weary travelers. Christian sat down to rest and read his roll for comfort. Pleased, he fell asleep, and the roll slipped from his hand.

When it was almost night, someone found Christian sleeping and startled him from sleep, saying: "Go to the ant, you sluggard; consider its ways and be wise!"

Ashamed, he scrambled all the way to the top of the hill. Two men rushed toward him. "Sirs, what's the matter that you run the wrong way?" cried Christian.

"We were on our way to the Celestial City, but the farther we go, the more danger we meet with," said a man called Timorous. "Therefore we turned around to go back."

"Before us were a couple of lions," said the other man, Mistrust. "We don't know if they were awake or asleep. But we were afraid that if we came within their reach, they would rip us to pieces."

"You make me afraid too," said Christian. "But where would I flee for safety? Going back to my own country is sure death. It is destined for fire and brimstone, and I will certainly die there. If I can but get to the Celestial City, I am sure to be safe. So to go back is nothing but death. Going ahead is fear of death, and beyond it, everlasting life! I will go forward."

Timorous and Mistrust scurried down the hill. Thinking about what they had told him, Christian felt for his roll for comfort, and he discovered it was gone. In great distress, he tried to think where he might have lost it. Then he remembered falling asleep in the arbor. He fell on his knees and asked God to forgive him for his foolish sleeping. Then he went back to look for his roll, bewailing his sinful sleep: "Oh, what a wretch I am!"

On the way he looked on each side of the path in case it had fallen on the way. Back at the arbor, his sorrow renewed. "How could I sleep in the daytime? Why did I sleep in the midst of difficulty? Why did I indulge the flesh self-ishly and take advantage of the arbor the Lord of the Hill erected only for the relief of pilgrims? What a waste of time that I should walk this part of the path three times over, when I should only have done it once!"

Finally he looked under the settee where he sat, and he spied his roll. He picked it up and placed it into his breast pocket for safekeeping.

Who could know his joy at finding his rolled certificate? It was the assurance of his life, acceptance at the Celestial Gate. He thanked God for directing his eye to the roll.

Nevertheless, he went on his way, nimbly climbing the hill once again. But when the sun set, he bewailed his bad fortune that had him walking in the dark. He remembered the story that Timorous and Mistrust had told him about the lions.

Suddenly, he saw ahead a stately palace beside the way. He rushed ahead, hoping to get lodging there. He entered a very narrow passage leading to the porter's lodge, and saw the two lions just ahead. Afraid, he thought of turning around as Timorous and Mistrust had. For now nothing but death was before him. He stopped. Should he go back?

The porter at the lodge, whose name is Watchful, saw that Christian had stopped, and shouted to him. "Is your strength so small? Don't fear the lions. They are chained and are there to test the genuineness of your faith. Keep in the middle of the path, and you will not be harmed."

Trembling, Christian went past the lions. He heard their roars, but they did him no harm. Then he clapped his hands and ran to the porter's gate. "Sir, what palace is this?" he cried to the man who had yelled encouragement.

"This Palace Beautiful was built by the Lord of the Hill for the relief and security of pilgrims," Watchful answered. "Where are you from and where are you going?"

"I come from the City of Destruction, and I'm going to the Celestial City."

"What is your name?"

"My name is now Christian, but my name at first was Graceless."

"The sun is set. Why are you so late?"

After Christian recounted his foolishness in losing his roll, the porter said, "I will call out one of the virgins. If she likes your talk, she will take you in to the rest of the family." He rang a bell.

Out came a beautiful but very serious maiden named Discretion.

"This is Christian, and he is on his way from the City of Destruction to the Celestial City. He has asked for lodging here tonight. After you have talked with him, you can do what seems best, even according to the law of the house."

She asked him many questions. Finally she smiled with tears in her eyes. She called out several more members of her family: Prudence, Piety, and Charity. They, too, questioned him before inviting him into the palace, saying, "Come in, you who are blessed. The Lord of the Hill built this palace for us to entertain the pilgrims along the way."

Then he bowed his head and followed them into the palace. He sat down, and they gave him something to drink. The four women decided to question Pilgrim further while they waited for supper.

Piety asked, "What moved you at first to become a pilgrim?"

"The fear that unavoidable destruction awaited me." And Christian went on to describe his journey.

"But how did it happen that you came out of your country this way?"

"It was under God's control. When I was under the fear of destruction, I didn't know where to turn. But by chance Evangelist sought me out, and he directed me to the wicket gate where I found the way."

"Didn't you come by the house of the Interpreter?" Piety asked.

"Yes," Christian said. "And I saw many things there that will stick with me as long as I live."

"What else have you seen along the way?"

"I went a short way from the Interpreter's house, where I saw One hanging and bleeding on a cross. The very sight of him made my burden fall off my back."

Piety asked Christian a few more questions about the things he'd seen along the way.

Then Prudence asked him, "Do you not yet bear some worldly desires?"

"Yes, but greatly against my will. My carnal impulses are now my grief," Christian answered. "I would love to never think of these things again. But when I want to do the best things, that which is worst is with me."

"What is it that makes you desire to go to the Celestial City?" asked Prudence.

"Why, I hope to see Him alive who did hang dead from the Cross. I hope to be rid of all those things in me that to this day are an annoyance. There they say there is no death. To tell you the truth, I love Him because He eased my burden. I am weary of my inner sickness. I long to be where I shall never die, with the company that shall continually cry, 'Holy, Holy, Holy is the Lord God Almighty.'"

Charity asked, "Aren't you a married man?"

"I have a wife and four boys."

"Why did you not bring them along with you?"

Weeping, Christian said, "Oh, how I wish I had! But they were against my going on pilgrimage."

"But you should have talked to them and tried to have shown them the danger of being behind," Charity persisted.

"I told them what God had showed to me of the destruction of our city. But I seemed to them as one that mocked, and they believed me not."

"And did you pray to God that He would bless your counsel to them?"

"Yes, and that with much affection, for you must know that I love my wife and children very much."

"Did you tell them of your own sorrow and fear of destruction?"

"Over and over and over. But still I was unable to persuade them to come with me."

"But what reason did they give for not coming with you?"

"My wife was afraid of losing this world, and my children loved the foolish delights of youth. So they left me to follow this path alone. I know I'm not perfect, but nothing I did or said could persuade them to join me."

After that they sat down to a supper of rich food and fine wine. All their talk was about the Lord of the Hill. They saw Him as a great warrior who had fought and slain he who had the power of death. He did it with the loss of much blood. But that which put glory of grace into all that He did was that He did it from pure love. Some in the household said they had seen Him since He died on the Cross, and no greater love of poor pilgrims was to be found from the east to the west. Thus they talked until late at night.

After they prayed and asked their Lord for protection, they went to bed. Christian slept in a large upper chamber of the Palace Beautiful called Peace.

In the morning he awoke to the rising sun and sang:

"Where am I now? Is this the love and care
Of Jesus, for the men that pilgrims are,
He did provide? That I should be forgiven,
And dwell already the next door to heaven!"

❧

His hosts told him he shouldn't leave until they had showed him the rarities of the palace. In the study they showed him the pedigree of the Lord of the Hill, that He was the Son of the Ancient of Days, from an eternal generation. Here also were recorded more fully the acts He had done, and the names of many hundreds He had taken into His service. Then they read some of the worthy acts His servants had done, how they had "conquered kingdoms, administered justice, and gained what was promised; who shut the mouths of lions, quenched the fury of the flames, and escaped the edge of the sword; whose weakness was turned to strength; and who became powerful in battle and routed foreign armies."

Then they read testimonies that showed how willing their Lord was to receive into His favor all mankind, even though in time past they had offered great affronts to His person and working. There also were several other histories that spoke of things both ancient and modern, together with accounts of the fulfillment of certain prophecies and predictions that brought fear upon His enemies and comfort to His pilgrims.

The next day they took him into the armory

and showed him all kinds of armor the Lord had provided for pilgrims: sword, shield, helmet, breastplate, prayer, and shoes that would not wear out. There was enough to outfit as many men for the service of the Lord as there are stars in the heavens. They also showed him Moses' rod; the hammer and nail with which Jael slew Sisera; the trumpets, pitchers, and lamps with which Gideon put to flight the armies of Midian; the ox's goad Shamgar used to slay six hundred men; the jawbone with which Samson fought; the sling and stone with which David killed Goliath; and the sword their Lord will use to kill the Man of Sin in the last days.

On the third day, Christian planned to take up his pilgrimage once more. But the day was clear, and they took him to the top of the palace to show him the view. They told him to look south. When he did, he saw a most pleasant mountainous country in the distance, with woods, vineyards, fruits of all sorts, flowers, and springs and fountains.

"What country is this?" Christian asked.

"Emmanuel's Land," they said. "It is as well known as the Hill of Difficulty for all pilgrims. When you get there you'll be able to see the gates of the Celestial City. Any of the shepherds there will be happy to show you."

Again, Christian desired to be on his way.

"But first," his hosts said, "let us go again to the armory." And there they outfitted him from head to foot with armor, to protect him should he meet with assaults on the way.

Thus equipped, Christian walked with his friends Discretion, Piety, Charity, and Prudence down the hill.

As they passed the porter at the gate, Christian asked, "Have you seen any pilgrims pass by the gate?"

"Yes," the porter replied.

"Did you know him?"

"He told me his name is Faithful."

"Oh, I know him," Christian said. "He is a fellow townsman, a near neighbor, from the place where I was born. How far ahead of me is he?"

"He should be at the bottom of the hill by now."

So Christian and his friends went on together till they came to the where the path started downhill.

"It appears to be as dangerous going down as it was coming up," he said.

"Yes," said Prudence. "It is hard for a man to go down into the Valley of Humiliation without tripping. That is why we are going with you."

So Christian began the downhill trek very carefully. Yet he still slipped once or twice.

At the bottom of the hill his good companions gave him a loaf of bread, a bottle of wine, and a sack of raisins.

And Christian went his way.

Christian had gone but a little way in the Valley of Humiliation when he spied a foul fiend coming over the field to meet him. Afraid, Christian anxiously thought about whether to turn back or to stand his ground. But when he realized he had no armor for his back and to turn around would give the fiend the greater advantage to pierce him with his darts, he resolved to stand his ground.

So he went on until the fiend stood before him. The monster was hideous to behold. Scaled like a fish, he had wings like a dragon and feet like a bear. Out of his belly came fire and smoke. His mouth was fanged like a lion.

The fiend looked down on Christian with disdain. "Where do you come from? And where are you going?" demanded the monster.

"I come from the City of Destruction, which is a place of evil, and I am going to the Celestial City."

"By this I perceive you are one of my subjects, for all that evil country is mine. I am Apollyon, the prince and god of that land. Why have you run away from your king? Were it not for the hope that you may do me more service, I would strike you now with one blow to the ground."

"I was born in your dominions, but your service was hard, and your wages were not enough for a man to live on. 'For the wages of sin is death.' So I want to heal myself. I am going to the Celestial City."

"No prince will so lightly lose his subjects. Since you complain about my service and wages, go back to the City of Destruction. What my country can afford, I promise to give you."

"I have given myself to the King of Princes. How can I go back with you?"

"You have done according to the proverb, and exchanged bad for worse. But it is very common for those who have professed themselves His servants to return to me. If you do so as well, all shall be well."

"I have given Him my faith and sworn my allegiance to Him. How can I go back from this and not be hanged as a traitor?"

"You did the same to me," Apollyon said. "Yet I am willing to forget it all if you will turn again and go back."

"What I promised to you was done when I was too young to know better. The Prince under whose banner I now stand is able to absolve me and pardon all I did in compliance to you. Besides, I like His service, His wages, His servants, His government, His company, and His country better than yours. Therefore, leave me alone. I am His servant, and I will follow Him."

"Reconsider your ways with a cool head. Do you not know how many of His servants have been put to shameful deaths? Besides, He never came personally to deliver any who served Him in my country. Yet how many times have I delivered, either by power or fraud, those who have faithfully served me? In the same way will I deliver you."

"He waits to deliver them purposefully, to try their love, whether they will stay with Him to the end. As for the bad end you say they come to, that is glory to their account. His servants don't expect immediate deliverance, preferring to wait until the Prince does come in His glory."

"You have already been unfaithful to Him. Why would you think He will pay you wages for that?"

"When have I been unfaithful to Him?" demanded Christian.

"You almost choked in the Slough of Despond. You tried various ways to rid yourself of your burden when you should have waited until your Prince took it off. You sinfully slept and lost your roll. You almost turned back at the sight of the lions. And when you speak of your journey and what you have heard and seen along the way, you inwardly desire praise in all you say and do."

"All that is true, and much more. But the Prince I serve is merciful and ready to forgive."

Then Apollyon broke out in a terrible rage. "This Prince is my enemy. I hate His person, His laws, and His people. I have come out on purpose to stand against you."

"Apollyon, beware what you do, for I am in the King's highway, the way of holiness. Therefore, take heed to yourself."

Then Apollyon straddled the way. "I am unafraid in this matter. Prepare to die." He threw a flaming spear.

Christian blocked it with his shield. Then spears came as thick as hail. Christian had wounds on his head, hand, and foot. He backed up and Apollyon followed. Christian again took courage and resisted as best he could. The combat lasted half a day, Apollyon roaring hideously the whole time. Christian grew weaker and weaker.

Sensing his opportunity, Apollyon rushed Christian to wrestle him. Christian fell, and his sword flew from his hand.

"I am sure of victory now," roared Apollyon.

But as Apollyon drew back for his last blow, Christian's groping hand found his sword. "Do not gloat over me, my enemy! Though I have fallen, I will rise." With that he gave Apollyon a deadly thrust, which made him stumble back as one who had received a mortal blow.

Christian came at him again, saying, " 'Nay, in all these things we are more than conquerors through Him that loved us.' "

When the monster saw Christian ready to thrust again, he spread his wings and sped away.

When the battle was over, Christian said, "I will give thanks to Him who has delivered me out of the mouth of the lion." In gratefulness, he sang:

"Great Beelzebub, the captain of this fiend,
Designed my ruin; therefore to that end
He sent the fiend out harnessed, in a rage,
So hellish he did fiercely me engage:
But blessed Michael helped me, and I,
By dint of sword, did quickly make him fly:
To Michael's help, let me give lasting praise,
And thank, and bless His holy name always."

❧

Then came to him a hand with leaves from the Tree of Life. Christian applied them to his wounds, and they healed immediately. He ate the bread and drank the wine that had been given to him at the Palace Beautiful. Then, sword drawn, he left the valley to enter another: the Valley of the Shadow of Death!

Christian had to go through this valley because the way to the Celestial City lay through the middle of it. The prophet Jeremiah described it as a wilderness, a land of deserts and of pits, a land of drought and of the shadow of death, a land that no man but a Christian passes through, a land where no man dwells.

When Christian arrived at the border of the valley, two men ran toward him. "Back! Back!" they cried. "If you prize either life or peace."

"What have you met with?" asked Christian.

"Why, the valley itself, which is dark as pitch. We also saw hobgoblins, satyrs, and dragons of the pit. We heard continual howling and yelling of people in unspeakable misery, bound in irons. Overhead hang clouds of confusion. Death hovers everywhere. It is dreadful—utter chaos."

"But it is the only way to my desired haven," Christian said.

"Fine for you, but we will not choose it for ours," the men said before they parted from Christian.

So Christian went on, with his sword drawn in his hand in case he should be assaulted. On his right hand yawned a very deep ditch, into which the blind had led the blind for all ages. On his left hand there was a very dangerous quagmire with no bottom. The pathway here was very narrow, making it difficult for Christian to stay out of the ditch on the right and the quagmire on the left. Christian sighed bitterly when he frequently encountered such darkness that he could not see where to place his feet as he moved forward.

Soon he came closer to flames and smoke shooting out in such abundance, with sparks and hideous screams, that his sword was no good now. He had another weapon: prayer. He continued on for a long way with the flames reaching toward him. He heard many mourning voices, rushing feet, so that he thought he might be torn in pieces or trodden down in the streets. He cried, "I call 'on the name of the Lord': Oh Lord, save me!"

Coming to a place where he thought he heard a pack of fiends creeping toward him, he stopped. He had half a thought to go back, but knew the danger of going back might be more than the danger of going forward. Yet the fiends came nearer and nearer.

He cried out in a fiery voice, "I will walk 'in the strength of the Lord'!"

The fiends disappeared.

But now Christian was so confused he did not know his own voice. After he passed the burning pit, one of the wicked ones stepped behind him. The fiend suggested wicked blasphemies to Christian, making him believe they came from his own mind. Distressed to think that he could now blaspheme the One he loved so much before, he knew that if he could have helped it, he would not have done it.

After some considerable time, he thought he heard a voice ahead: "Even though I walk through the Valley of the Shadow of Death, I fear no evil, for You are with me."

Christian calmed. Someone else who feared God was in this valley whom he hoped to meet soon. And God was with him. As he walked on, he called to him he had heard but received no answer. When morning came, Christian looked back into the dark to see what he'd gone through. He was deeply moved by his deliverance from such dangers.

Yet as the sun was rising, he could see the valley before him was, if possible, far more dangerous. The way was full of snares, traps, and nets here, and full of pits, steep slopes, and deep holes there. Had it been as dark as it had been the first part of the way, a thousand souls would have been lost there.

Christian said, "His lamp shines upon my head, and by His light I walk through darkness."

In this light Christian came to the end of the valley. At the end of this valley lay blood, bones, ashes, and mangled bodies of men who had gone this way before.

Then he sang:

"Oh, world of wonders! (I can say no less)
That I should be preserved in the distress
That I have met with here! Oh, blessed be
The hand that from it has delivered me!
Dangers in darkness, devils, hell, and sin
Surrounded me while I was in this glen:
Yes! Snares and pits and traps and nets did lie
About my path, so worthless silly I
Might have been snared, entangled, and
    cast down:
But since I live, let Jesus wear the crown."

∽

Now as Christian topped a small rise, he saw ahead of him a pilgrim.

Christian yelled, "Wait up, and I will be your companion."

Faithful looked behind him but did not stop. So Christian called again for him to wait.

But Faithful called back: "I cannot pause—the Avenger of Blood is behind me."

Christian exerted himself and ran him down. As he went ahead of Faithful, Christian tripped and fell and couldn't rise again until Faithful came up to help him.

Christian said, "I am glad that I have overtaken you and that God has so changed our spirits we can be companions on this pleasant path."

"I had hoped, dear friend, to have your company directly from our town. But you got the start on me. Therefore, I was forced to come this far of the way alone."

"How long did you stay in the City of Destruction before you set out after me?"

Faithful said, "Until I could stay no longer. There was much talk in town about your desperate journey, for that is what they call your pilgrimage. But I believed, and still do, fire and brimstone from above will destroy our city. Therefore, I made my escape."

"Did you hear no talk of neighbor Pliable?"

"He has been had in great derision. Hardly anyone will give him work. He is seven times worse off than if he had never gone to the Slough of Despond. People mock and despise him as a turncoat!"

"But why are they so against him, since they also despise the way that he forsook?"

"They call him a turncoat, saying he was not true to his profession. I think God has stirred up even his enemies to hiss at him and make him a proverb because he has forsaken the way."

"Did you talk to him before you left?"

"He crosses the street to avoid me. He is ashamed of what he did. So I never spoke to him."

"Well, when I first set out, I had hopes of that man. But now I fear he will perish in the overthrow of the city. For it has happened to him according to the true proverb, 'A dog returns to its vomit.' But let us leave him and talk of things that more immediately concern ourselves. What have you met on the way?"

"I escaped the slough that I heard you fell into, and got to the gate without that danger. I was sorely tempted by a woman named Wanton at the wicket gate, but I went my way."

"What did she do to you?"

"You cannot imagine what a flattering tongue she had. She promised me all manner of content if I would turn aside."

"But she did not promise you the content of a good conscience."

"No, so I shut my eyes so that I would not be bewitched with her looks. Then she scolded me, and I went away."

"Did you meet with no other assault as you came?"

"When I came to the foot of the Hill of Difficulty, I met an old man named Adam the First. He lives in the town of Deceit and offered to pay me if I would live with him. I asked him what work he had for me, and he said his work was many delights. And he would make me his heir. He offered me his three daughters: Lust of the Flesh,

Lust of the Eyes, and Pride of Life. And I was inclined to go until I saw written on his forehead: PUT OFF THE OLD MAN WITH HIS DEEDS. And it came burning into my mind that he was going to make me a slave. So when I refused and pulled away, he pinched me so hard I thought he had a piece of my flesh. When I got halfway up the Hill, a man overtook me and beat me until I thought I was dead. He said he served Adam the First."

"That was Moses," said Christian. "He does not know how to show mercy to those who break the Law."

"Yes. He would doubtless have killed me, if someone had not stopped him."

"And who was that?"

"I did not know Him at first, but soon saw the holes in His hands and side. I was saved by the Lord of the Hill."

"Did you see the Palace Beautiful?"

"Yes, and the lions, too, but they were asleep. However, because I had so much of the day before me, I passed by the porter and came down the hill."

"He told me about it. But I wish you had called at the palace. They would have showed you so many rarities that you would scarce have forgotten them to the day of your death. Who did you meet in the Valley of Humiliation?" asked Christian.

"I met Discontent. He told me the valley was without honor. And if I were to wade through this valley, I would offend all our friends: Pride, Arrogance, Self-Conceit, and Worldly Glory. I told him they were indeed relatives of mine, for they are according to the flesh. But since I became a pilgrim, they disowned me. And I reject them. Moreover I told him he had misrepresented the valley, because before honor is humility and a haughty spirit before a fall. Therefore, I told him, I'd rather go through this valley to the honor received from the Wise One than choose that which Discontent esteemed most worthy of our affections."

"Who else did you meet?"

"Shame. He said religion is a pitiful, low, sneaking business for a man to care about, a tender conscience is unmanly, and a man who watches his words and ways is to be ridiculed. He also said that few of the mighty, rich, and wise were ever of this opinion. It is shameful to repent or make restitution after a sermon. It is shameful to ask forgiveness for a petty fault. Religion alienates a man from the great because of a few vices, though he called those vices by much finer names."

"What did you say?"

"At first I couldn't think of what to say. Then I remembered that which man holds in high esteem is an abomination to God. I said he only told me what men are. He told me nothing about God or the Word of God. On the Day of Judgment, life and death are not determined by the world but by God's wisdom and law. So what God says is best, even though all men in the world reject it. So I told him to leave me because God prefers His Word and a tender conscience, declares those who make themselves fools for the kingdom of heaven as truly wise, and makes the poor man who loves Christ richer than the greatest man in the world. I said he was an enemy to my salvation, and I refused to have anything to do with him. But still he attempted to point out other weaknesses of religion. At last I told him that it was useless for him to continue with his accusations because in those things he disdained, I saw the most glory. And when I was rid of him at last, I sang:

> "The trials that those pilgrims meet withal,
> Who are obedient to the heavenly call,
> Are many kinds and suited to the flesh,
> And come, and come, and come again afresh.
> So now, or sometime else, we by them may
> Be taken, overcome, and cast away.
> Oh, let the pilgrims, those astride the way,
> Be vigilant, behave like saints today."

∽

"I'm glad you withstood the villain so bravely," said Christian. "I think he has the wrong name. He attempts to make pilgrims ashamed before all men, but he has no shame in his audacity. He promotes the fool. The wise will inherit glory, but shame promotes fools."

"We must cry to Him for help against Shame, for He would have us be valiant for truth upon the earth."

"Well said," Christian said. "Who else did you meet in the valley?"

"No one. I had sunshine all the rest of the way through the Valley of Humiliation, and also through the Valley of the Shadow of Death."

Christian then spoke of his battle with Apollyon and the darkness in the Valley of the Shadow of Death.

The path became very wide, and walking beside them was a man who at first appeared tall and handsome, yet became homelier the closer he got to them.

"Are you going to the Heavenly Country?" called Faithful.

"The same place," answered the man.

"May we have your good company? We will talk of things that are profitable."

"To talk of things that are good is very acceptable to me," answered the man. "With you or anyone else. I'm glad that I have met with those who desire such a good thing. Too many talk of things of no profit. This is a problem for me."

"I agree it is a problem," Faithful said. "For what is a worthier use of men's tongues and mouths than the things of the God of heaven?"

"I like you very well, for your speech is full of conviction. I will add, what is so profitable as to talk of the things of God? What things are so pleasant? And if a man loves to talk of the history or the mystery of things, miracles, wonders, or signs, where shall he find things so sweetly penned as in the Holy Scripture?"

"That's true," Faithful replied. "We should strive to gain profit from such things in our conversations."

"As I said, to talk of such things is most profitable. A man may get knowledge of many things, such as the emptiness of earthly things and the benefit of things above. More particularly, by conversation a man may learn the necessity of the new birth, the insufficiency of good works, and the need of Christ's righteousness. A man may learn what it is to repent, to believe, to pray, to suffer, or the like. By this also, a man may learn what are the great promises and consolations of the Gospel, to his own comfort. Even more, a man may learn to refute false opinions, to vindicate the truth, and also to instruct the ignorant."

"All this is true, and glad am I to hear these things from you."

"Indeed, few understand the necessity of a work of Grace in their soul in order to gain eternal life, but live ignorantly in the works of the Law, by which no man can obtain the kingdom of heaven."

"By your leave," added Faithful, "heavenly knowledge such as this is the gift of God. No man can hope to attain them by works or only the talk of them."

"All this I know very well. For a man can receive nothing except it be given him from heaven. All is of grace, not of works. I could give you a hundred scriptures to confirm this truth," the man replied.

"So what is the one thing that we shall talk about at this time?"

"Whatever you want. I will talk of heavenly or earthly things, moral or evangelical, sacred or profane, past or future, things foreign or domestic, essential or circumstantial," the man said. "Provided that all that is said or done is for our profit."

At this, Faithful began to wonder about their companion, and turning to Christian, he whispered, "What a brave companion have we got? Surely this man will make a very excellent pilgrim!"

Christian smiled and said, "This man, with whom you are so taken, will beguile twenty strangers with his tongue."

"Do you know him?" asked Faithful.

"Better than he knows himself."

"Who is he, then?"

"His name is Talkative," Christian answered. "He dwells in our town. I'm surprised that you don't know him."

"Who is his father? Where in town does he live?"

"He is the son of Say-Well. He lived in Prating-Row. He's well known in that part of town. In reality, he's a pitiful man, in spite of his glib tongue."

Faithful said, "Well, he seems to be a very pleasant fellow."

"He is to those who don't know him well. He reminds me of the work of the Painter, whose pictures show best at a distance but unpleasing when viewed close at hand."

"I think you must jest, because you smiled just now."

"God forbid that I should jest in this matter or that I should accuse any falsely. Talkative adapts to any company or talk. He talks as well in a tavern. He has no religion in his heart or his home. They are as empty of religion as the white of an egg is of flavor. Religion is only on his tongue."

"Then I am greatly deceived."

"Remember: 'The kingdom of God is not a matter of talk but of power.' This man talks of prayer, repentance, faith, and the new birth. But he knows only to talk of them. I have been in his family and have observed him both at home and about town. What I say of him is the truth. His house is as empty of religion as the white of an egg without flavor. He neither displays any indication he prays or repents of his sin. Talkative is the shame of religion. A brute serves God better than he.

"The people who do know him say he is 'a saint abroad, and a devil at home.' I know his family finds that proverb true. He is so rude and unreasonable his servants have no idea how to do their jobs or speak to him. Men who have had business dealings with him say that he goes beyond all others in fraud, deception, and unscrupulous behavior. And he's bringing up his sons to be as him. He has caused many men to stumble and fall. And if God doesn't prevent it, he will be the ruin of many more."

Said Faithful, "I am inclined to believe you, not only because you say it but also because you've made this report as a Christian man. I can't imagine why you would say these things out of ill will."

"If I hadn't known him, I might have thought of him as you first did," Christian assured his friend. "In fact, if the enemies to religion had given this assessment of Talkative's character, I would have thought it slander. But all I have spoken about him I can prove him guilty of. Good men are ashamed of him because they can call him neither brother nor friend. Just his name makes them blush if they know him."

"Well, I see that saying and doing are two things. From now on I will better observe this distinction."

"The very soul of religion is the practical part: 'Pure religion and undefiled before God and the Father is this, To visit the fatherless and widows in their affliction, and to keep himself unspotted from the world.' But Talkative thinks that hearing and saying will make a good Christian. He deceives his own soul. Hearing is just the sowing of the seed, and talking is not sufficient to prove that the fruit of the seed is in the heart and life. The end of the world is compared to our harvest with our fruit. There nothing can be accepted that is not of faith."

"I am not fond of him now. What shall we

do to be rid of him?" Faithful asked.

"Take my advice, and do as I bid you," Christian answered. "You will find that he'll be sick of your company, too, unless God touches his heart and turns it."

"What shall I do?"

"Go to him and enter into some serious discourse about the power of religion. Ask him plainly whether religion is set up in his heart, house, or conversation."

Then Faithful called to Talkative, "How does the saving grace of God manifest itself, when it is in the heart of a man?"

"So we speak about the power of things? It's a very good question, and I'm happy to answer you. First, where the grace of God is in the heart, it causes a great outcry against sin. Secondly—"

"Wait a moment," interrupted Faithful. "I think it shows itself by inclining the soul to abhor its sin."

"Why, what's the difference between crying out against sin and abhorring sin?"

"Oh, a great deal: A man may cry out because of a law against it, but he cannot abhor it unless he has a godly antipathy against it. What was your second point?"

"Great knowledge of the gospel mysteries."

"That is also false. Great knowledge may be obtained in the mysteries of the gospel and yet not work as grace in the soul. Consequently he would not be a child of God. A man may know like an angel, and yet be no Christian; therefore your sign is not true. Indeed, to know is a thing that pleases talkers and boasters; but to do is that which pleases God. Not that the heart can be good without knowledge, for without that, the heart is nothing. There is therefore knowledge and *knowledge*— knowledge that rests in the bare speculation of things, and knowledge that is accompanied with the grace of faith and love—which puts a man upon doing even the will of God from the heart. The first of these will serve the talker, but without the other, the true Christian is not content. If a man 'can fathom all mysteries and all knowledge' but has not love, he is nothing," countered Faithful. "What is another point?"

"None. I see we shall not agree."

"Well, if you won't give another point, will you give me permission to do it?"

"You may use your liberty."

"A work of grace in the soul shows, either to him who has it or to others who observe it. To the one who has it, it gives him conviction of sin, especially whatever defiles his nature and the sin of unbelief. Because of his sinful condition and the battle between it and grace, he finds the Savior of the world revealed in him. According to the strength or weakness of his faith in his

Savior, so is his joy and peace and love for holiness, as well as his desire to know Him more
and to serve Him in this world. Others see in his
life an inner abhorrence to sin, a desire to pro-
mote holiness in the world, not by talk only but
by a practical subjection in faith and love to the
power of the Word. Now, sir, if there is anything
you object to in what I've spoken, please do so.
If not, then give me permission to offer a second
question for discussion."

"My part is not to object now, but to hear.
Let me have your second question."

Faithful said, "It is this: Do you experience
the first part of the description of it? And does
your life and conversation testify the same? Or is
your religion based in word or conversation, and
not in deed and truth? Please, if you decide to answer me in this, say no more than you know the
God above will say Amen to and also nothing but
what your conscience can justify in you."

Talkative flushed angrily. "You now speak
of experience, conscience, and God, and to ap-
peal to Him for justification of what is spoken.
This kind of discourse I did not expect, nor am
I disposed to give an answer to such questions,
because I'm not bound by it. I refuse to make
you my judge. But please tell me why you ask me
such questions."

"Because of your willingness to talk, and

because I didn't know if you had anything else but empty words. Besides, to tell you all the truth, I have heard of you that you are a man whose religion lies in talk, and that your conversation gives your mouth-profession the lie. They say that religion fares the worse for your ungodly conversation, that some already have stumbled at your wicked ways, and that more are in danger of being destroyed because of your words. The proverb is true of you, which is said of immoral women: She is a shame to all women. So you are a shame to all followers."

"Since you are ready to listen to gossip and to judge so rashly as you do, I cannot but conclude that you are some irritable, dismal man. You are not my judge. You are not fit to be talked to. Good-bye."

Christian joined Faithful. "I told you how it would happen. Your words and his lusts could not agree. He would rather leave your company than reform his life. But he is gone. Let him go," said Christian. "The loss is no one's but his own. He has saved us the trouble of leaving him. Besides, the Apostle says, 'From such withdraw thyself.'"

Faithful said, "I am glad we have had this conversation with him. It may happen that he will think of it again. I have dealt plainly with him and so am clear of his blood if he perishes."

"You did well to talk so plainly as you did.

Men to whom religion is only a word make religion stink in the nostrils of many," said Christian. "I wish all such men could be dealt with as you have dealt with Talkative. Religion would enter their hearts, or the company of saints would be too hot for them."

Faithful sang:

"How Talkative at first lifts up his plumes!
How bravely does he speak. How he
    presumes
To overwhelm all minds near! But as soon
As I did speak of heart, like waning moon,
He shrivels to an ever smaller part:
And so do all, but those who know the
    heart."

ಉ

Thus they talked of what they had seen on the way, and so made the way easy, instead of tedious. For now they went through wilderness. They were almost out of the wilderness when they saw someone coming after them.

"It is my good friend Evangelist," said Christian.

"And mine, too," said Faithful, "for he showed me the way to the gate."

"Peace be with you, dearly beloved," called Evangelist, "and peace be with your helpers."

"Welcome, my good Evangelist," Christian said. "Seeing you brings to my remembrance your ancient kindness and unwearied labor for my eternal good."

"And a thousand times welcome," said Faithful. "Your company, O sweet Evangelist, is beneficial to us poor pilgrims!"

"How has it fared with you, my friends, since our last parting? What have you met with, and how have you behaved yourselves?"

Christian and Faithful told him of all the things that had happened to them on the way.

"Right glad I am," said Evangelist, "that you have been victors. The day is coming when both he who sows and they who are reaped shall rejoice together. The crown is before you, and it is an incorruptible one. So run that you may obtain it. Be careful that no one comes in and takes it from you. Hold fast. You are not out of gunshot of Beelzebub. Let the kingdom be always before you and believe steadfastly concerning things that are invisible. Let nothing that is on this side of the other world get within you. And above all, look well to your own hearts and to the lusts thereof, for they are deceitful above all things, and desperately wicked. Set your faces like a flint. You have all power in heaven and earth on your side."

Christian said, "We well know you are a

prophet. Tell us what is going to happen to us."

"My sons, you have heard in the words of the truth of the gospel that you must go through many tribulations to enter into the kingdom of heaven. And that in every city, bonds and afflictions abide in you. You cannot expect that you should go long on your pilgrimage without them, in some sort or other. You have found something of the truth of these testimonies upon you already, and more will immediately follow. For now, as you see, you are almost out of this wilderness. You will soon come into a town, and you will be beset with enemies who will strain hard to kill you. One or both of you will seal your testimony with blood. But be faithful unto death, and the King will give you the crown of life. He who shall die there, although his death will be unnatural and his pains perhaps great, will arrive at the Celestial City sooner and escape many miseries of the rest of the journey. So when you are come to the town and shall find fulfilled what I have here related, then remember your friend, and quit yourselves like men, and commit the keeping of your souls to your God, as unto a faithful Creator."

When Christian and Faithful came out of the wilderness, they entered the town of Vanity. The town had kept a fair the year around and called it Vanity Fair because the town is lighter than vanity and everything sold at the fair is vanity.

Almost five thousand years ago, Beelzebub, Apollyon, and Legion with their companions set up the fair because Vanity was on the way to the Celestial City. At the fair, pilgrims could find houses, lands, trades, places, honors, promotions, titles, countries, kingdoms, lusts, pleasures, and delights of all sorts—whores, wives, husbands, children, masters, servants, lives, blood, bodies, souls, silver, gold, pearls, precious stones, and whatnot. To be seen were juggling, games, plays, fools, apes, knaves, and rogues. And for nothing there were thefts, murders, adulteries, cheats, and slanders. Every pilgrim to the Celestial City had to go through this town. Even the Prince of Princes went through the town to His own country. Beelzebub would have made Him Lord of the fair, would He have revered him as He went through the town. He was such a person of honor the devil showed Him all the kingdoms of the world that he might entice Him to cheapen and buy some of his vanities. But the Blessed One left Vanity without spending one penny.

Christian and Faithful entered the city, and they attracted intense interest. Their garments were like none other at the fair, made out of material that couldn't be found there. The people watched them closely, casting judgment. Some said they were fools, some called them madmen, and others said they were from a strange place.

Their speech set them apart from the people of Vanity, and only a few could understand them. They naturally spoke the language of Canaan, holy things, but those who kept the fair were men of this world. As they walked past the many booths, Christian and Faithful didn't even look at the wares. When someone called on them to buy, they put their fingers in their ears and cried, "Turn away my eyes from seeing vanity." They kept their gazes upward, and they indicated their trade and wares were in heaven.

On seeing the way Christian and Faithful carried themselves through the town, one seller mockingly said, "What will you buy?"

But they looked gravely at him and said, "We buy the Truth."

At that, many openly despised the pilgrims the more—some mocking, some taunting, some speaking reproachfully, and some calling upon others to smite them. The confusion in the fair was so great, all order was destroyed. Word reached Beelzebub, who quickly came down and had some of his most trusted friends bring in the men for interrogation.

Those who examined them asked, "Where did you come from? Where are you going? And why are you in Vanity, wearing such unusual clothing?"

Christian and Faithful said they were pilgrims going to their heavenly Jerusalem. They hadn't given any reason to the men of the town or the sellers at the fair to ridicule them, except to say, when asked what they would buy, that they would buy Truth.

The interrogators did not believe them and said the two were either madmen or troublemakers. They beat them and smeared them with dirt. They put them in a cage, so they would be a spectacle at the fair. They lay for some time and were made the objects of any man's sport, malice, or revenge, laughing still at all that befell them.

The two remained patient, giving good words for bad, kindness for injuries.

Some less prejudiced people at the fair thought the men were treated unfairly. Angered, the merchants let fly at their accusers again, counted them as bad as the men in the cage, and told them that they seemed allies and should be made partakers of their misfortunes. The other replied that for all they could see, the men were quiet and sober and intended nobody any harm. They pointed out that there were many who traded in their fair who were more worthy to be put into the cage, and pillory, too, than were the men they abused. Thus, after many words had passed on both sides, they fell to some blows among themselves and did harm one to another.

Even though Christian and Faithful were quiet and calm throughout the fights, they were again brought before their examiners for more questioning. They were charged with being guilty of the latest hubbub in the fair. So the two poor men were beaten and marched in leg irons to terrorize the others, lest any more should further speak in their behalf or join them. But Christian and Faithful behaved themselves yet more wisely and received the humiliation and shame that was put on them with such meekness and patience that it won to their side several of the men in the fair.

This put the other party yet into a greater rage, insomuch that they concluded the death of these two men. Wherefore they threatened that neither cage nor irons should serve their turn, but that they should die for the abuse they had done, and for deluding the men of the fair. This time they were threatened with death. So they were sent back to the cage and their feet put into stocks until further order should be taken with them.

While they remained in the cage, they remembered what they had heard from their faithful friend Evangelist, and they were the more confirmed in their ways and sufferings because of what he told them would happen to them. They also now comforted each other, that whose lot it was to suffer, even he should have the best; therefore each man secretly wished that he might have that advancement. But contentedly committing themselves to Him who rules all things, they lived in the condition in which they were until they should be otherwise disposed of.

On the day that was set, they were brought to trial before their enemies and arraigned. They were indicted on these charges: that they were enemies to the people and disturbers of their trade; that they were the cause of the civil unrest and divisions in the town; and that they had followers to their most dangerous opinions in contempt of the law of their prince.

Judge Hate-Good made Faithful the first prisoner of the bar.

In answer to the charges against him, Faithful said that he had only set himself against that which had set itself against Him who is higher than the Highest. "As for disturbance, I make none, being myself a man of peace. The followers who chose to follow us were won by beholding our truth and innocence and are only turned from the worse to the better. As for the king you speak of, since he is Beelzebub, the enemy of our Lord, I defy him and all his angels."

Then a proclamation was made that they who had anything to say for their lord the king against the prisoner at the bar should come forward with their evidence. Then three witnesses were sworn in: Envy, Superstition, and Opportunist. They were then asked if they knew the prisoner at the bar and what they had to say for their king against him.

Envy testified first. "My lord, I have known this man a long time. This man is one of the vilest men in our country. He has no regard for prince or people, law or custom. He does all he can to persuade all men of his principles of faith and holiness. I heard him say Christianity and the customs of our town are diametrically opposite, and could not be reconciled. By which saying, my lord, he does at once condemn not only all our laudable doings, but also us in the doing of them. I could say much more, but I don't want to bore the court. If any charge be lacking, I will be glad to enlarge my testimony against him."

The judge requested him to stand by until the rest of the testimony was heard.

Superstition was then called and testified. "I have no great acquaintance with this man, nor do I desire to have further knowledge of him. However, I do know that he is a pestilent fellow from some of the discourse I had with him the other day in this town. I heard him say that our religion was nothing and that it could by no means please God. In fact, his saying was that the people of Vanity worship in vain, are in sin, and shall be damned!"

Then the third witness was sworn in and testified. "I have known this fellow for a long time," said Opportunist. "I have heard him speak things that ought not be spoken. He not only has railed against our noble Prince Beelzebub, but also has spoken contemptibly of our prince's honorable friends the Lord Carnal-Delight, the Lord Luxurious, the Lord Vain-Glory, my old Lord Lechery, and Sir Greedy. Moreover, he has said that if all men were of his mind, there is not one of these noblemen should have any place in this town. He has not been afraid to rail on you, my lord. He called you, Judge, an ungodly villain and many other vilifying terms."

"Renegade! Heretic! Traitor!" yelled Judge Hate-Good to Faithful. "Have you heard the charges by these honest gentlemen?"

"May I speak a few words in my defense?" asked Faithful.

"You don't deserve to live any longer and you will be slain immediately after the proceedings. Yet, so all men may see our gentleness to you, let us hear what you have to say."

"In answer to Envy's charge, I only said that any prince or people or law or custom against the Word of God is also against Christianity. If this is spoken amiss, convince me of my error, and I am ready to recant before you. As to Superstition's charge, I said that in the worship of God there is required a divine faith, but there can be no divine faith without a divine revelation of the will of

God. Therefore, whatever is thrust into the worship of God that is not agreeable to divine revelation cannot be done but by a human faith which will not profit to eternal life. Finally, in response to Opportunist, ignoring the part where he said I 'railed,' I say that the prince of this town along with all the rabble, the attendants Opportunist named, are more fit for hell than for this town and country. Lord, have mercy on me."

Then the judge spoke to the jury. "Gentlemen of the jury, you see this man about whom so great an uproar has been made in this town. You have also heard what these worthy gentlemen have witnessed against him. Also you have heard his reply and confession. It now lies in your breasts to hang him or save his life, but I think it appropriate to instruct you in our law.

"There was an act made in the days of Pharaoh, servant to our prince, that in case those of a contrary religion should multiply and grow too strong for him, their males should be thrown into the river. There was also an act made in the day of Nebuchadnezzar, another of his servants, that whoever would not fall down and worship his golden image should be thrown into a fiery furnace. There was also an act made in the days of Darius, that whoever called upon any God but him should be cast into the lions' den. Now the substance of these laws this rebel has broken, not only in thought but also in word and deed.

"Pharaoh's law was made to prevent mischief, no crime being yet apparent; but here is a crime apparent. For the second and third, you see he disputeth against our religion, and for the treason he has confessed. He deserves to die."

Then the judge sent the jury out. In its chamber they deliberated. Everyone gave his private verdict against Faithful among themselves, and afterward they unanimously concluded to bring him in guilty before the judge.

The jury foreman, Blind-Man, said, "I see clearly this man is a heretic."

No-Good said, "Rid the earth of this fellow."

"I hate the very looks of him," agreed Malice.

Love-Lust added, "I could never endure him."

"Nor I," Live-Loose said. "He would always be condemning my ways."

"Hang him. Hang him," reasoned Brainy.

High-Mind muttered, "A sorry scrub indeed."

"My heart is black toward him," snarled Enmity.

"He is a rogue," said Liar.

Cruelty insisted, "Hanging is too good for him."

Hate-Light said, "Let's get rid of him."

Implacable had the final opinion: "If I had all the world given to me, I could not be reconciled to him. Let's vote him guilty of death."

Therefore Faithful was condemned to be put to the cruelest death that could be invented.

They therefore brought Faithful out to punish him according to their law. First, they scourged him. Then they beat him. Then they stabbed him with knives. After that they stoned him. Then they slashed him with swords. Then they burned him to ashes at the stake. Thus, Faithful died.

Unseen to the multitude, a chariot and a couple of horses stood behind the crowd, waiting for Faithful. As soon as he died, Faithful was put in the chariot and was carried up through the clouds to the sound of trumpets and off to the Celestial Gate.

Christian was given a short reprieve and sent back to prison where he remained for a while. And He who rules all things brought it about that Christian escaped his cage.

And Christian left Vanity mourning:

"Well, Faithful, you have faithfully professed
Unto your Lord, with Him you shall be blessed;
When faithless ones, with all their vain delights,
Are crying out under their hellish plights:
Sing, Faithful, sing, and let your name survive;
For though they killed you, yet are you alive."

∽

As Christian fled Vanity, a man named Hopeful

joined him. And hopeful he was, made so by beholding the words and behavior of Christian and
Faithful in their sufferings at the fair. Thus, one
died testifying to the truth; another rose from his
ashes to accompany Christian in his pilgrimage.
Hopeful told Christian many more people at the
fair would follow on the pilgrimage, but it would
take time.

The two pilgrims soon overtook a man.
"How far do you go this way? And where are
you from?" they asked.

"I'm going to the Celestial City. I'm from
the town of Fair-Speech."

"Fair-Speech?" Christian asked. "Is there
any good that lives there?"

"Yes," the man said. "I hope."

"What is your name, sir?" Christian asked.

"I am a stranger to you and you to me. If
you're going this way, I shall be glad of your
company. If not, I must be content."

Christian said, "This town of Fair-Speech,
I have heard of it. As I remember, they say it's a
wealthy place."

"Yes, it is," the man agreed.

"Who are your relatives there?"

"Almost the whole town. I have many rich
relatives there. In particular Lord Turn-About,
Lord Time-Server, and Lord Fair-Speech himself. Also Smooth-Man; Facing-Both-Ways;

Anything, the parson of our parish; and Two-Tongues, my mother's brother. To tell the truth, I have become a gentleman of good quality. And to think my grandfather was just a waterman, looking one way and rowing another. I earned most of my wealth in the same way."

"Are you married?" Christian asked.

"Yes, and my wife is a very virtuous woman from a very honorable family, daughter of Lady Feigning. My wife has arrived at such a fineness of breeding that she knows how to maintain her composure with every social level from prince to peasant. It's true we differ in religion from those of a stricter sort, yet only on two small points. First, we never strive against wind and tide. Secondly, we are most zealous when religion goes in his silver slippers. We love to walk with him in the street, if the sun shines and people applaud him."

Then Christian stepped closer to Hopeful to speak to him privately. "I'm pretty sure that this is By-Ends of Fair-Speech. If so, we have as deceitful a man with us as dwells in all these parts."

Hopeful said, "Ask him. I don't think he should be ashamed of his name."

Christian turned to the other man and asked, "Sir, you talk as if you knew something more than all the world does. And I believe I know who you are. Is not your name By-Ends?"

"That is not my name. It is a nickname given

to me by those who cannot stand me. I must be content to bear that reproach. I never gave an occasion to earn the name."

"But did you never give a reason for men to call you by this name?"

"Never! Never! The worst that ever I did to give them a reason was that I have always been lucky, that's all. I count it a blessing, and don't allow the malicious to reproach me."

"I thought indeed that you were the man that I've heard of. However, I believe this name belongs to you more properly than you are willing to believe."

"Well, I can't help what you think. You'll still find me fair company, if you will still accept me as your associate."

"If you go with us, you must go against wind and tide, which is against your opinion. And you must be loyal to religion in rags as well as silver slippers. You must be ready to stand by him whether he is bound in irons or walks the streets with everyone's applause."

"You must not impose your faith," said By-Ends, "nor lord it over my faith. Let me go with you in freedom."

"Not a step farther, unless you will do as we believe," said Christian.

"I won't desert my principles, since they are harmless and profitable. If I can't go on with you, then I will go on by myself. I'll wait until someone comes along who will be glad of my company."

So Christian and Hopeful left By-Ends behind and kept their distance ahead of him. But before long, they noticed that three men following By-Ends came up with him. The men gave him a very low bow in greeting. By-Ends welcomed them since they were former schoolmates: Hold-the-World, Money-Love, and Save-All. Their schoolmaster had taught them the art of getting either by violence, fraud, flattery, lying, or religion.

Money-Love said to By-Ends, "Who are they upon the road before us?"

"They are a couple of far countrymen who are going on pilgrimage according to their own way."

"Why did they not stay that we might have had their company? Are we not all on the same pilgrimage?"

"We are, indeed," said By-Ends. "But the men in front of us are so rigid and so love their own notions and lightly esteem the opinions of others that if a person doesn't believe the same way in all things, they thrust him out of their company."

Save-All spoke: "That's bad. But we read of some who are overly righteous. Such rigidness makes them judge and condemn all but themselves. But in what did you differ?"

"They conclude that it is their duty to keep going on the way in all weather, and I wait for wind and tide. They are willing to hazard all for God, while I am for taking all advantages to secure my life and estate. They will hold their beliefs even if everyone is against them, but I am for religion that is in keeping with the times and doesn't hazard my safety. They are for religion that will keep them in poverty and makes them hold in contempt all others. However, I am for him when he walks in his golden slippers in the sunshine and gives me praise."

Hold-the-World said, "Stay with your beliefs, By-Ends. Those men are fools who, having liberty to hang on to the pleasures of this world, instead let go of them. Let us be content to take the fair weather with us and not the rain. I like that religion best that will give us the security of God's blessing. Why would God withhold any good thing from us and keep them for Himself?"

With that, the four men agreed with one another and spoke no more of the two men in front of them.

By-Ends then asked innocently, "Then let's look for a better diversion from things that are bad. Suppose a minister or a tradesman had an opportunity to get the good blessings of life, but only if he had to become very zealous on some point of religion he never bothered with before. May he not get the blessings and still be an honorable man?"

Money-Love spoke right away: "I see what you are getting at, and I'm willing to shape an answer. Let's take the minister first. If he can benefit from such a small alteration of principle, I see no reason why he can't do it and still be an honest man. After all, the desire for blessings is lawful and the opportunity is set before him by Providence. Besides, his desire makes him a more studious, a more zealous preacher and a better man before God. His people won't mind if he denies to serve them some of his principles. That will prove he has a self-denying temperament and a sweet and winning personality, making him even more fit for the ministry. So I conclude that a minister who changes a small for a great should not be judged as covetous, but rather, since he is improved in his parts and industry, he pursues his call and the opportunity to do good.

"Now as to the tradesman, suppose such a one has a poor business, but by being religious, he can improve his market, maybe even get a rich wife. I see no reason why this is not lawful. To become religious is a virtue. Nor is it unlawful to get a rich wife. By becoming good himself, he gets a good wife and good customers and good profit."

The others applauded Money-Love for a wholesome and advantageous answer. They decided that because Christian and Hopeful were still within sight and hearing they would ask them the same question. So they called after the two men before them, who stopped and waited for them.

After greeting the two men, Hold-the-World gave out the original question. Then he asked, "What do you think, Christian?"

"A babe in religion could answer that. Only heathens, hypocrites, devils, and witches would make Christ and religion a stalking-horse to get worldly riches. To answer the question affirmatively, as I perceive you have done, and to accept as authentic such an answer is heathenish, hypocritical, and devilish. Your reward will be according to your works."

With that reprimand, the four men grew sullen and fell behind.

"If they cannot stand before a man, how will they stand before God? And if they are mute when dealt with by vessels of clay, what will they do when they shall be rebuked by the flames of a devouring fire?" asked Christian.

Christian and Hopeful went far ahead until they came to a narrow plain called Ease to come to a hill called Lucre. In that hill was a silver mine, which because of its rarity had lured many pilgrims to leave the path to investigate it. But the ground around it was not stable, and the pilgrims fell into the pit and perished. Those who didn't die bore permanent injuries and could not be their own selves again.

A man at the side of the road called to them, "Come over here, and I will show you a silver mine. With a little sweat, you may get rich."

"Let us go and see," said Hopeful.

"Not I," said Christian. "I have heard of this place. Many have died here. And the treasure is a snare to those who seek it, for it keeps them from their pilgrimage." And he called to Demas, "Is not the place dangerous?"

"Only to those who are careless," answered the man, blushing.

Christian said to Hopeful, "Let's not stir a step but keep on our way."

"I'll guarantee you that if By-Ends receives the same invitation, he will turn aside to see," said Hopeful.

"No doubt," Christian agreed. "His principles will lead him that way, and he will die there."

The man called out again, "But will you not come over and see?"

"You are an enemy to the righteous ways of the Lord, Demas," called Christian. "And you have already been condemned by one of His Majesty's judges for your own turning aside. Why do you seek to bring us into like condemnation?"

"But I also am a pilgrim. If you will wait a little, I will walk with you."

"Is not your name Demas?" Christian asked.

"Yes, that is my name. I am the son of Abraham."

"I know you," Christian said. "You have trod in the steps of Gehazi and Judas. It is an evil prank you use. Your father was hanged for a traitor, and you deserve no better reward. Be assured that when we come to the King, we will give Him word of your behavior."

So Christian and Hopeful went on their way. And Christian sang:

"By-Ends and Silver Demas both agree;
One calls, the other runs, that he may be
A partner in his Lucre; thus such fools
Are lost in this world that the devil rules."

∽

The pilgrims came to a place where a monument stood by the side of the way. When they saw it, they were both disturbed, for it seemed as if a woman had been transformed into a pillar. Hopeful saw written above the head the words REMEMBER LOT'S WIFE.

Christian said, "This comes opportunely after the invitation from Demas."

"I am sorry I was so foolish. I wonder, what difference is there between her sin and mine? She only looked back, and I had a desire to go see. Let grace be adored, and let me be ashamed that ever such a thing was in my heart."

"Let us take notice of what we see here for our help for time to come. This woman escaped one judgment, the destruction of Sodom. Yet she was destroyed by another."

"True, and she may be to us both caution and example—caution that we should shun her sin; example to beware. But above all this, I wonder how Demas and his fellows can stand so confidently yonder to look for that treasure when this woman, just for looking behind her, was turned into a pillar of salt. Especially since she stands within sight of where they are. They can't help but see her if they look up."

"It is something to wonder about. It argues that their heart is grown desperate in this case. It is said of the men of Sodom that they were sinners exceedingly because they were sinners before the Lord. That is, in His eyesight and notwithstanding the kindnesses that He showed them, they provoked Him the more to jealousy and made their plague as hot as the fire of the Lord out of heaven could make it. It leads to the conclusion that despite such visible examples set continually before them to caution them to the contrary, they must be partakers of the severest of judgments."

"What a mercy it is that I myself was not made this example," Hopeful said. "She is a caution to both of us. We should thank God, fear Him, and always 'remember Lot's wife.'"

They went on their way and soon reached a pleasant river. It seemed David's River of God, John the Baptist's Water of Life. Their way lay on the bank of this river, and they walked with great delight. The pilgrims drank of the water, which was pleasant and enlivening to their weary souls. On both banks of the river were green trees with all kinds of fruit. The leaves of the trees were good for medicine, and the fruit was delicious. On either side of the river was a meadow, beautified by lilies. It was green all year long. Here they slept safely. When they awoke, they gathered fruit and drank the water of the river. This they did for several days and nights.

They sang:

"Behold, you, how these crystal streams do glide
To comfort pilgrims by the highway side.
The meadows green besides their fragrant
*   smell,*
Yield dainties for them: And he who can tell
What pleasant fruits and leaves these trees do
*   yield,*
Will soon sell all, so he can buy this field."

When Christian and Hopeful decided to continue

on their way, they ate and drank and left the peaceful meadow. They had not journeyed far when the river and the path they followed parted. They were sorry to leave the river behind, but they dared not go out of the way. However, the way from the river was rough and their feet were tender because of their travels. So the souls of the pilgrims were discouraged, and they wished for a better way.

A little way ahead of them, on the left side of the road, was By-Path Meadow. In the meadow a path went along the way.

"Why shouldn't we walk over there?" asked Christian as he climbed onto the stile to look into the meadow. "Come, Hopeful, that path is easier going."

"But what if the path should lead us out of the way?"

"That's not likely. Does the path not parallel the way?"

So they crossed a stile that spanned the fence and walked the path in the meadow. Ahead of them walked a man. Christian called, "Who are you? And where does this path go?"

"I'm Vain-Confidence. This path goes to the Celestial City," replied the man.

"Didn't I tell you so?" Christian asked Hopeful.

When night came, it grew very dark, and they could no longer see the man ahead.

Vain-Confidence, not seeing the way before him, fell into a deep pit, which was on purpose there made by the prince of those grounds to catch fools in it. He was dashed in pieces with his fall.

But the pilgrims heard him fall, then heard only groaning. So they called out to know what was the matter, but no one answered.

"Where are we now?" asked Hopeful. "Let's stop."

But Christian was silent, afraid that he had led Hopeful out of the way. Now it began to rain and thunder and lightning in a dreadful way. Water rose around them.

Hopeful groaned and cried, "Oh that I had kept on my way!"

Christian answered, "Who could have thought that this path should have led us out of the way?"

"I was afraid of it from the very first and therefore gave you that gentle caution. I would have spoken plainer, but you are older than I."

"Good brother, be not offended. I am sorry I have brought you out of the way and that I have put you into such imminent danger. Please forgive me. I didn't do it with evil intent."

"Be comforted, my brother, for I forgive you. And I believe that this shall be for our good."

"I am glad I have with me a merciful brother. But we must not stand here. Let's try to go back again."

"Let me go before," Hopeful offered.

"No, let me go first, so that if there is any danger, I will be the first one in. It's my fault that we are both gone out of the way."

"No, you shall not go first, for your mind is troubled, and it may lead you out of the way again."

Then they heard a voice say, "Let your heart take you to the way again."

By this time the waters were very high, and the way of going back was very dangerous. Even so, they tried to go back. But it was so dark and the flood so high that they could have drowned nine or ten times.

So at last they found a little shelter, and they sat down to wait for day to break. Being tired, they fell asleep. Not far from the place where they were lay a castle. The owner, Giant Despair, got up early that morning, and while walking his grounds, he caught Christian and Hopeful asleep on his grounds.

With a grim and surly voice he woke them. "Where are you from and what are you doing on my land?"

"We are pilgrims who have lost their way."

"You are trespassing by trampling in and lying on my grounds of Doubting Castle! You must come with me."

Despair was a giant! So they were forced to go because he was stronger than they. They also had but little to say, for they knew themselves to be at fault.

He prodded them to his castle, where he threw them down into a very dark dungeon, nasty and stinking. Here they lay from Wednesday morning until Saturday night, without one bit of bread or drop of drink or light or any to ask how they did. Far from friends and acquaintances, no one knew where they were. In this place, Christian had double sorrow because it was his unadvised haste that brought them here.

When Despair went to bed, he told his wife, Diffidence, what he had done and how the two prisoners in his dungeon had gotten there. When he asked for her advice, she counseled him to beat the prisoners without mercy.

So when he arose the next morning, he got a large crabtree cudgel and went down to the dungeon to them. There he cudgeled them fearfully, so that they were unable to help themselves. When Despair was done, he withdrew and left them there to their misery.

All that day they spent the time in nothing but sighs and bitter lamentations.

When Diffidence learned that the pilgrims still lived, she advised Despair to counsel his prisoners to do away with themselves. So in the morning, he went to the dungeons irritated. He saw they were very sore from the beating.

"Why live?" asked Despair. "Life holds only bitterness. I'll give you a choice of a knife, a rope, or poison."

They begged the giant to let them go, but seized by a fit brought on by sunshine, he threw them back in the dungeon and withdrew.

Christian said, "What shall we do, brother? The life we now live is miserable! As for me, I don't know whether it is best to live this way or to die. My soul chooses strangling by rope rather than life. The grave is easier for me than this dungeon! Shall we be ruled by the giant?"

"Indeed our present condition is awful, and death would be far more welcome to me than to live like this forever. But yet the Lord of the country to which we are going has said, 'You shall not murder,'" replied Hopeful. "And for one to kill himself is to murder body and soul at once. And have you forgotten the hell that awaits murderers? Also, think of this. Not all the law is in the hand of the giant Despair. Others have been taken by him, as well as we, and they have escaped out of his hands. Who knows but that God, who made the world, may cause the giant to die, or that at some time or other he may forget to lock us in? Or he may have another of his fits before us and may lose the use of his limbs. If that ever happens again, I am resolved to pluck up my courage and try my utmost to get from under his hand. I was a fool that I did not try to do it before. However, my brother, let's be patient and endure awhile. The time may come that we will find a happy release. But let us not be our own murderers." With that, Hopeful changed Christian's mind.

As evening drew near, the giant went down into the dungeon again to see if his prisoners had taken his counsel. But when he got there, he found them alive. Barely. They'd had no bread or drink in all the time they'd been there, and with the wounds they received from their beating, they could do little more than breathe. Despair fell into a terrible rage and told them that since they had disobeyed his counsel, it would be worse with them than if they had never been born.

At this the pilgrims trembled greatly, and Christian fell into a swoon. When he came a little to himself again, they renewed their discourse about the giant's counsel and whether they should take it or not. Christian seemed to be for doing it again, but Hopeful tried to dissuade him again.

"My brother, do you remember how valiant you have been before now? Apollyon could not crush you, nor could all that you heard or saw or felt in the valley of the Shadow of Death. What hardship, terror, and consternation you have already gone through, and are you now nothing but fear? You see that I am in the dungeon with you, a far weaker man by nature than you are; also, this giant has wounded me as well as you, and has also cut off the bread and water from my mouth, and with you I mourn without the light. But let's exercise a little more patience. Remember how you played the man at Vanity Fair, and were neither afraid of the chain nor cage, nor yet of bloody death. Let us at least avoid the shame that a Christian shouldn't bear and hold up with patience as well as we can."

That night after the giant and his wife were in bed, she asked him concerning the prisoners, and if they had taken his counsel.

He replied, "They are sturdy men who choose to bear all hardships rather than to make away themselves."

Then said she, "Take them into the castle yard tomorrow and show them the bones and skulls of those that you have already killed, and make them believe that before a week comes to an end, you also will tear them in pieces, as you have done their fellows before them."

The next day Despair took them into the castle yard and showed them bones and skulls of his victims. "These were pilgrims who trespassed on my grounds as you have done. I tore them into pieces. Within ten days I will tear you apart, just as I have done to these pilgrims before you." And he beat them all the way back into the dungeon.

All day Saturday they lay in the dungeon in a horrible state.

That night in bed, the giant and his wife again discussed the fate of the prisoners. The giant wondered that he could not bring them to an end no matter what he did.

His wife replied, "I fear that they live in hope that some will come to relieve them, or that they have picklocks about them which they hope will help them escape."

"Now that you mention it, my dear, I will search them in the morning."

At midnight on Saturday they began to pray, and they prayed until just before daybreak.

A little before daybreak, Christian, half stunned at a sudden thought, said, "What a fool I've been to lie in this stinking dungeon when I could walk away free! I have a key in my bosom called Promise that is supposed to open any lock."

"That is good news, brother. Pluck it out of your bosom and try."

Christian used his key to unlock the door to the cell, then the door to the castle yard, then the great iron gate to the castle. But that lock was very hard. It did open. But when they thrust open the gate, it creaked so loudly, Despair ran out in the sunshine to pursue them; but he was seized by a fit, and his limbs were too weak to allow him to give chase.

The men ran all the way back and found the stile that led to the way again. Once over the fence they were out of the giant's jurisdiction, and therefore were safe. To prevent other pilgrims from making their mistake, they erected a pillar with a warning: "Over this stile is the way to Doubting Castle, which is kept by Giant Despair, who despises the King of the Celestial City and seeks to destroy His holy pilgrims." That done, Christian and Hopeful continued on the way, singing:

> *"Out of the way we went, and then we found*
> *What it was like to tread forbidden ground.*
> *And let those who come after note today,*
> *Lest carelessness makes them, too, leave the*
> *way,*
> *Lest they, for trespassing, his prison bear,*
> *Whose castle's Doubting, and whose name's*
> *Despair."*

❧

They went until they came to the Delectable

Mountains. They climbed up into the mountains to see gardens and orchards, vineyards, and fountains of water. They drank and washed themselves and freely ate of the vineyards. At the tops of the mountains by the side of the road, four shepherds were feeding their flocks.

Christian and Hopeful went to them, and as they leaned on their staves, Christian asked, "Whose Delectable Mountains are these? And whose sheep feed upon them?"

"These mountains are Emmanuel's Land," answered a shepherd. "They are within sight of His City. These sheep belong to Him. He laid down His life for them."

"Is this the way to the Celestial City?"

"You are in your way," the shepherd agreed.

"How far is it to get there?" Christian asked.

"Too far for all but those who persevere."

"Is the way to the Celestial City safe or dangerous?" asked Christian.

"Safe for some. 'But the rebellious stumble' in the way."

"Is there in this place any rest for the weary?"

A shepherd replied, "The Lord of these mountains told us, 'Do not forget to entertain strangers.' Therefore the good of the place is yours."

Then the four shepherds asked Christian and Hopeful many questions, such as, Where did you come from? How did you get into the way? By what means have you so persevered in your journey? They saw few pilgrims, because most didn't make it that far. When the shepherds heard their answers, they were pleased and looked lovingly on them.

"Welcome to the Delectable Mountains," said one. "We are Knowledge, Experience, Watchful, and Sincere." They took Christian and Hopeful by the hand and led them to their tents. They made them eat of that which was ready at the moment.

And they said, "We would like you to stay here awhile, to come to know us, and most importantly to be comforted with the good of these Delectable Mountains."

Christian and Hopeful said they were content to stay. They all went to bed soon after that because it was very late.

The next day the shepherds took them walking. They had a pleasant view to behold on every side. Then the shepherds decided to show them some wonders. So they first took them to the top of the mountain called Error, which was very steep on its far side. When the shepherds bid them to, the pilgrims looked down a precipice to see several men dashed to pieces from a fall they had from the top.

"What happened?" asked Christian.

"These men listened to Hymenaeus and Philetus, who said the resurrection of the faithful had already taken place," answered a shepherd. "They lie unburied from that day until now as a warning to take heed how they clamber too high or how they come too near to the brink of the mountain."

Next they topped the mountain of Caution. In the distance they saw men walking up and down among the tombs that were there. And they saw the men were blind because they stumbled against the tombs and never found their way out of the graveyard.

"What does this mean?" asked Christian.

A shepherd answered, "Did you see a little below these mountains a stile that led into a meadow on the left-hand side of the way?"

"Oh yes."

"From that stile there goes a path that leads directly to Doubting Castle, which is kept by Giant Despair, and these men came on the pilgrimage at one time, as you do now, until they came to the stile. Because the path is rough in that spot, they chose to go out of it into the meadow and were carried off by the giant and cast into the dungeons at the castle. He ripped out their eyes and led them among those tombs to wander to fulfill the proverb: 'A man who strays from the path of understanding comes to rest in the company of the dead.'"

Then Christian and Hopeful looked at one another with tears streaming down their faces, but yet said nothing to the shepherds.

Next the shepherds led them into a valley where there was a door in the side of a mountain. As one shepherd opened the door, they bid the pilgrims to look in. When they did, they saw that within it was very dark and smoky. They also thought that they heard a rumbling noise as of fire and a cry of some of the tormented. The odor of smoke and brimstone nearly overwhelmed them.

"What is it?" asked Christian.

"A detour to hell," answered a shepherd. "For hypocrites, mainly, like Esau, who sold his birthright; or like Judas, who sold his Master; or like Alexander, who blasphemed the Gospel; or like the liars Ananias and Sapphira."

"Each one had started the pilgrimage like us, did they not?" asked Hopeful.

"Yes," said the shepherds. "And held it a long time, too."

"How far might they go on pilgrimage in their day, since they were thus miserably cast away?" asked Hopeful.

"Some farther, and some not so far as these mountains."

"Then we have need to cry to the Strong One for strength."

"Ay, and you will have need to use it when you have it," agreed the shepherds.

By this time, the pilgrims had a desire to go forward on their journey. So the shepherds walked them to the end of the mountains, intending to show the pilgrims the gates of the Celestial City. On the mountain of Clear they let the pilgrims look toward the Celestial City through a telescope.

As they tried to look, the remembrance of the last thing the shepherds had shown them made their hands shake so they could not look steadily through the glass. Yet they thought they could make out something like the gate and some of the glory of the place.

As they departed, one of the shepherds gave them a "Note of the Directions of the Way."

Another cautioned, "Beware of the Flatterer."

The third warned, "Take heed not to sleep on the Enchanted Ground."

The fourth bid them, "Godspeed!"

Then they went away, singing this song:

"Thus by the shepherds secrets are revealed,
Which but for pilgrim eyes are kept
concealed:
Come to the shepherds, then, if serious

To see things hidden and mysterious."

❧

The pilgrims headed down the mountains along the way toward the City. A little below the mountains on the left hand lay the country of Conceit. From that country there comes into the way in which the pilgrims walked a little crooked lane. Here they met with a very energetic lad who came out of that country. His name was Ignorance.

"From what land do you come?" called Christian. "And where do you go?"

"I am Ignorance," replied the lad. "I come from Conceit. I'm going to the Celestial City."

"You may have some difficulty there getting in the Gate."

"As other good people do," answered Ignorance.

"But what rolled certificate do you have to show at the Gate?"

"I know my Lord's will," replied Ignorance. "I have lived a good life. I pay my debts. I pray, fast, pay tithes, give alms. And I have left my country for the Celestial City."

"But you didn't come in at the wicket gate that is at the head of the way," worried Christian. "I fear you will not get into the City. Instead you will be charged 'a thief and a robber.' "

"Gentlemen, you are utter strangers to me. I don't know you. Be content to follow the religion of your country, and I will follow the religion of mine. I hope all will be well, and as for the wicket gate that you talk of, all the world knows that it is a great way off. I cannot think that any men in all our parts do so much as know the way to it. Nor need it matter whether they do or not, since we have, as you see, a fine pleasant green lane that comes down from our country the way into it."

When Christian saw that the man was wise in his own conceit, he whispered to Hopeful, "There is more hope of a fool than of him. As Solomon the wise man says, 'Even as he walks along the road, the fool lacks sense and shows everyone how stupid he is.' Shall we talk further with him now or go ahead of him and leave him to think about what he's already heard? Later we could join up with him and see if by degrees we can do him any good."

"Let us pass him and talk to him later, if he can bear it," said Hopeful. "It is not good, I think, to say all to him at once."

So they went on and Ignorance stayed behind them on the way. When they had gotten ahead of Ignorance a ways, they entered a very dark lane. Off the way they saw a man bound by seven strong cords to a pole carried by seven devils. They carried him to a door set on the side of the hill. Christian began to tremble, as did Hopeful. As the devils led away the man, Christian looked to see if he knew him.

"The doomed man looks like Turn-Away from Apostasy," whispered Christian.

"Inscribed on the man's back are the words 'Wanton Professor and Damnable Apostate,'" whispered Hopeful.

"Now I remember something that was told me of a thing that happened to a good man hereabout," Christian said. "The name of the man was Little-Faith, but a good man, and he lived in Sincere. At the entrance of this passage there comes down from Broad-Way-Gate a lane called Deadman's Lane, so called because of the many murders that are commonly done there. Little-Faith was on pilgrimage, as we are now, and chanced to sit down there and fell asleep. About that time three men, sturdy rogues, came down that lane. They were three brothers, Faint-Heart, Mistrust, and Guilt. They saw Little-Faith where he was asleep and came running. Now the good man had just awakened and was getting up to continue his journey. The three came to him and with threatening language told him to stand. Little-Faith looked as white as a sheet and had neither power to fight nor fly.

"Faint-Heart said, 'Give me your purse,' but

Little-Faith made no haste to do it.

"Mistrust ran up to him and thrust his hand into his pocket and pulled out a bag of silver.

"At that Little-Faith cried out, 'Thieves, thieves!'

"Then Guilt, with a great club that was in his hand, struck Little-Faith on the head, and with that blow felled him to the ground where he lay bleeding.

"The thieves stood near until they heard someone on the road. Fearing that it might be Great-Grace who lives in the city of Good-Confidence, they ran away and left Little-Faith to fend for himself. After a while, Little-Faith came to himself and hobbled on his way."

"But did they take from all he ever had?" asked Hopeful.

"No. They missed the place where his jewels were. But, as I was told, the good man was much afflicted for his loss, for the thieves got most of his spending money. He had a little odd money left, but not enough to bring him to his journey's end. He was forced to beg as he went, to keep himself alive. Still he spent many times hungry all the rest of the way to the Celestial City."

"Is it not a wonder they didn't get his certificate by which he was to receive admittance at the Celestial Gate?"

"It is a wonder, but they didn't get it. Not

through his own cunning, for he hadn't any time to hide anything. So that was more of providence than his endeavor."

"But it must be a comfort to him that the thieves did not get that."

"It might have been a comfort to him if he had used it. But after the attack he made very little use of it the rest of the way because of the dismay that the thieves had got his money. In fact, he forgot most of the rest of his journey. Any memory that came to mind that comforted him, he lost when he had fresh thoughts of his loss. And those thoughts swallowed the comfort."

"Poor man! This could not be but a great grief to him."

"Ay, a grief indeed. It is a wonder he did not die with grief. I was told that he scattered almost all the rest of the way with nothing but doleful and bitter complaints."

"But, Christian, I am persuaded that these three fellows are a company of cowards. Otherwise would they have run as they did at the noise of one coming onto the road? And why didn't Little-Faith dig up some courage? I thought he might have stood up to them and yielded when there was no other choice."

"They are cowards. They are no better than journeymen thieves, serving under the king of the bottomless pit who will come to their aid if they need it. And his voice is like a roaring lion. When I was attacked by these three men, I, too, almost gave in when their leader roared. But I was dressed in the Armor of Proof. I still found it hard work to finish the work as a man."

"But they ran," Hope pointed out, "when they suspected that Great-Grace was coming."

"No marvel that they ran. Great-Grace is the King's champion. But put some space between Little-Faith and His champions. All the King's subjects are not His champions. Nor can they, when tried, do such feats of war as He. Some are strong, some are weak, some have great faith, some have little. This man was one of the weak; therefore he went to the walls.

"For such footmen as you and I are, let's never desire to meet with an enemy, nor vaunt as if we could do better when we hear of others who have been tricked and failed. But when we hear that such robberies are done on the King's highway, we have two things we can do: First, go out fully clothed in armor, including the shield; second, we must desire the King to go with us. Let us pray we can do better. Even Peter, who said he could stand firmer for his Master than all other men, was foiled by the villains."

So they went on with Ignorance following until they came to a place where they saw a way put itself into their way. It seemed to lie as straight as the way that they should go. They didn't know which of the two to take, for both seemed straight before them. So they stood still to consider.

A man in a white robe appeared on the other way.

"Where are you going?" he asked.

"To the Celestial City, but now we're not sure which is the right way," answered Christian.

"Follow me," said the man. "This is the way."

So they followed the man, who applauded everything the pilgrims said. Christian was confused. Did this new way ever so slowly depart from the way they had been on? Suddenly they were trapped inside a net, so entangled they didn't know what to do. The white robe fell off the man. He was a devil. And the pilgrims knew they were being led to hell. They lay crying for some time, for they could not get themselves out.

"Do you remember the proverb: 'Whoever flatters his neighbor is spreading a net for his feet'?" Christian asked Hopeful. "Did not the shepherds warn us about flatterers?"

"They also gave us a 'Note of Direction for the Way,' which we forgot to read," lamented Hopeful. "And now we are on the path of the destroyer."

They prayed for mercy. As they lay in the

net, a Shining One appeared, carrying a small whip. When he came to where they were, he asked where they came from and what they were doing there. They told him they were poor pilgrims on the way to the Celestial City. A devil in a white robe had tricked them out of the true way.

"It is Flatterer, a false apostle," said the Shining One. "He changes himself into an Angel of Light."

He ripped the net and let them out. Then he said, "Follow me that I may set you on your way again." So he led them back to the way.

Then he asked them, "Where did you lie last night?"

"With the shepherds upon the Delectable Mountains."

"Did they not give you a 'Note of Direction for the Way'?"

"Yes."

"But did you pull it out and read it when you were resting?"

"No."

"Why?"

"We forgot about it."

"Well then, didn't the shepherds tell you to beware of the Flatterer?"

"Yes, but we didn't even imagine that this fine-spoken man had been he."

But before the Shining One left them, he commanded them to lie down, and when they did he whipped them severely and scolded them for forgetting the directions of the shepherds. "As many as I love, I rebuke and chasten. Be zealous, therefore, and repent."

So they thanked the man for all his kindness, and as they continued carefully on the right way, they sang:

> *"Now listen, you who walk along the way,*
> *To hear how pilgrims fare who go astray:*
> *Ensnared they were, entangled in a net,*
> *Because good counsel did the two forget.*
> *It's true one rescued them, but yet you see*
> *He whipped them too: Let this your*
> *caution be."*

∽

After a while they saw a lone man coming carefully toward them.

Christian said to Hopeful, "There is a man with his back toward the Celestial City, and he is coming to meet us."

"I see him. Beware of another flatterer," whispered Hopeful.

So the man drew nearer and nearer, and at last came up to them.

"Where are you going?" asked the stranger.

"To the Celestial City," answered Christian.

The stranger laughed mightily. "What ignorant fellows you are, to take upon yourselves such a tedious journey. You'll get nothing for your pains, or my name isn't Atheist."

"Do you think we will not be received?"

"Received! There is no such place as you dream of in all this world."

"But there is in the world to come."

"I have been seeking this City for twenty years, but have found no more of it than the day I first set out."

"We both have heard and believe that there is such a place to be found."

"If I hadn't believed before I started out, I wouldn't have come this far to seek. But having found nothing, even though I should have if there was such a place, I'm going back again. I'll seek to refresh myself with the things I cast away before my fruitless quest."

"Do you think he speaks truth?" Christian asked Hopeful.

"Be careful," Hopeful said. "He is one of the flatterers. Remember what it has already cost us for listening to one of these fellows. What? No Celestial City? We saw the Gate of the City from the Delectable Mountains. We walk in faith. We are not of those who shrink back and are destroyed, but of those who believe and are saved. We will go on."

"My brother, I didn't ask the question because I doubted the truth of our belief myself, but to test you and to fetch from you a fruit of the honesty of your heart. As for this man, I know that he is blinded by the god of this world. Let you and I go on, knowing that we have belief in the truth and no lie is of the truth."

"Now I do rejoice in hope of the glory of God," Hopeful said.

And they turned away from the man. He laughed at them and went his way.

They went on the way until they entered a land whose air naturally tended to make one drowsy if he was a stranger in the land. Hopeful began to feel very dull and heavy of sleep. He said to Christian, "I am so drowsy. I can scarcely hold my eyes open. Let's lie down here and take a nap."

"By no means, unless you never want to wake up again," Christian said.

"Why, my brother. Sleep is sweet to the laboring man. We may be refreshed if we take a nap."

"Do you not remember the shepherds warning us of the Enchanted Ground? He meant that we should beware of sleeping. So let's not sleep as so many others do. Let us watch and be sober."

"I acknowledge my fault," Hopeful said. "Had I been here alone I might have died. The Wise Man said, 'Two are better than one.' Even before now, your company has been my mercy."

"Now then," said Christian, "to prevent drowsiness in this place, let us have a lively conversation."

"With all my heart."

"Where shall we begin?"

"Where God began with us, but you go first, please," said Hopeful.

So Christian sang this song:

"When saints grow sleepy, let them come to us,
And hear how lively pilgrims do discuss.
Yes, let them learn of what we did devise
To keep agape our drowsy, slumbering eyes;
Saints' fellowship, if it be managed well,
Keeps them awake, and that in spite of hell."

Then Christian said, "I will ask you a question. How came you to think at first of doing as you do now?"

"Do you mean, how came I at first to look after the good of my soul?"

"Yes, that is what I meant."

"I continued a great while in the delight of those things that are seen and sold at our fair, things that I now believe would have drowned me in perdition and destruction."

"What things were they?"

"All the treasure and riches of the world," Hopeful said. "Also I delighted much in revelry, partying, drinking, swearing, lying, uncleanness, Sabbath-breaking, and whatnot that tended to destroy the soul. But I realized at last, by hearing and considering of things that are divine, which indeed I heard from you and Faithful, that the end of these things is death. For these things the wrath of God comes on the children of disobedience."

"Did you presently fall under the power of this conviction?"

"No, I wasn't willing to know the evil of sin nor the damnation that follows on the commission of it. Instead I endeavored, when my mind at first began to be shaken with the Word, to shut my eyes against the light of it."

"But what was the cause of your carrying of it to the first working of God's blessed Spirit on you?"

"I was ignorant that this was the work of God on me. I never thought that my new awareness of sin was a result of God's seeking my conversion. Yet sin was very sweet to my flesh, and I didn't want to leave it. I didn't want to part with my old companions because their presence and actions were so desirable to me. But the hours when I was convicted of my sin were so trouble-some and frightening that I couldn't bear to re-member them."

"But sometimes you got rid of your trouble?"

"Yes, but it would come into my mind again, and it was worse than before."

"Before the journey, what brought your sins to mind?" Christian asked.

"Many things brought my sins to mind. If I met a righteous man in the street. If anyone read the Bible. If my head ached. If I heard a neighbor was sick. If I heard the bell toll for the dead. If I thought of dying myself. If I heard of someone else's sudden death. If I thought I my-self might come to sudden judgment."

"What did you do about it?" asked Christian.

"I endeavored to change my life. Not only turning away from my own sin, but putting the sinful company behind me, too. I prayed, read the Bible, wept for sin, and told the truth to my neighbors. But trouble returned."

"Why? Were you not reformed?"

"Several things brought it to me. Especially such sayings as 'All our righteousnesses are as filthy rags.' Because 'A man is not justified by Law, but by faith in Jesus Christ.' I finally came to the conclusion it was foolish to think of heaven by the law. If a man runs a hundred pounds into the shopkeeper's debt, and after that pays for all he buys, his old debt still stands in the shopkeeper's book unpaid. The shopkeeper may sue him and cast him into prison till he pays the debt."

"So how did you apply that to yourself?"

"Why, I thought this: I have by my sins run a great way into God's Book, and my now reforming will not pay off that score. Therefore I should think still, under all my present amendments. But how should I be freed from that damnation that I brought myself in danger of by my former sins?"

"A very good application."

"Another thing that has troubled me," Hopeful went on, "even since my late amendments, is that if I look narrowly into the best of what I do now, I still see sin, new sin, mixing itself with the best of that which I do. So now I'm forced to conclude that I have committed sin enough in one duty to send me to hell, even if my former life had been faultless."

"What did you do then?" Christian asked.

"I didn't know what to do until one day in Vanity I spoke my mind to Faithful. For we were well acquainted. He told me that unless I could obtain the righteousness of a man who had never sinned, neither my own nor all the righteousness of the world could save me."

"Did you think he spoke truth?"

"Not before I saw my own weakness to sin.

But since I've seen the sin that cleaves to my best performance, I've been forced to agree with him."

"But did you think, when at first he suggested it to you, that there was such a man to be found? Someone of whom it could truly be said, 'This man never committed sin'?"

"At first it sounded strange, but after a little more talk and time spent with Faithful, I had full conviction about it."

"Did you ask him, 'What man is this?' and how you must be justified by him?"

"Yes, and he told me it was the Lord Jesus who dwells on the right hand of the Most High. 'So,' he said, 'you must be justified by him, even by trusting to what He has done by Himself in the days of His flesh and suffered when He did hang on the tree.' I asked him how *that* Man's righteousness could be that powerful as to justify another before God. And he told me that He was the Mighty God, and He did what He did and died the death also, not for Himself but for me. His doings and their worthiness before God would be imparted to me if I believed on Him."

"What did you do then?" Christian asked.

"I listed my objections against my believing because I thought He was not willing to save me."

"What did Faithful say to you then?"

"He bid me to go to Him and see. I said that was presumption, and Faithful said no, I was invited to come. Then he gave me a copy of the Book of Jesus that spoke of His invitation to men, to encourage me to go to Him more freely. Then I asked Faithful what I must do when I came. And he told me I must pray on my knees with all my heart and soul, and the Father would reveal Him to me. Then I asked him what to say in my supplication when I came to Him, and Faithful taught me this prayer for salvation:

"God, be merciful to me, a sinner, and make me to know and believe in Jesus Christ. For I see that if His righteousness had not been, or I have not faith in His righteousness, I will be utterly cast away. Lord, I have heard You are a merciful God, and have ordained Your Son, Jesus Christ, the Savior of the world. Moreover, I have heard You are willing to bestow on such a poor sinner as I Your grace in the salvation of my soul, through Your Son, Jesus Christ. Amen."

"Did you do as you were bidden?"

"Yes, many times."

"Did the Father reveal His Son to you?"

"Not at first, nor for several times after that."

"What did you do then?"

"I didn't know what to do!"

"Had you thought of not praying anymore?"

"Oh yes. A hundred times and more."

"Why didn't you?"

"I believed that all was told me was true. I needed Christ's righteousness to live, and I thought if I quit praying for it, I would die in my sin. Then this verse came to mind: 'If it tarry, wait for it, because it will surely come, and it will not tarry.' So I continued to pray until the Father showed me His Son."

"How was He revealed to you?" asked Christian.

"One day I saw Him—not with my eyes but with my heart. The Lord Jesus looked down from heaven on me, saying, 'Believe in the Lord Jesus, and you will be saved.' And I replied, 'Lord, I am a very great sinner.' He answered, 'My grace is sufficient for you.' And my heart was full of joy, my eyes full of tears, my love running over in the ways of Jesus Christ. If I had a thousand gallons of blood in my body, I could spill it all for the sake of the Lord Jesus."

"This was a revelation of Christ to your soul indeed. But tell me specifically what effect this had on your spirit."

"It made me see that all the world is in a state of condemnation. It made me see that God the

Father, though He be just, can justify the sinner who comes to Him. I was greatly ashamed of the vileness of my former life, and I was confounded at the sense of my own ignorance. Until I saw the beauty of Jesus Christ, I didn't have love for the holy life. Now I long to do something for the honor and glory of the name of the Lord Jesus."

Just then Hopeful looked back and saw Ignorance. "Look how far the youngster loiters behind us."

"Ignorance does not care for our company."

"Let's wait for him."

When Ignorance came closer, Christian yelled, "Why do you stay so far behind?"

"I take greater pleasure walking alone," replied Ignorance.

"Come on up," Christian encouraged the young man. "Let us talk away the time in this lonely place. How do things stand between God and your soul?"

Ignorance drew closer. "I hope well, for I am always full of good thoughts that come into my mind to comfort me as I walk."

"What are these thoughts?"

"Of God and heaven."

"So do devils and damned souls," commented Christian.

"But I desire God and heaven," countered Ignorance.

"So do many who are never likely to go there. The soul of the sluggard desires and has nothing. Why are you persuaded you have left everything for God and heaven?"

"My understanding tells me so," said Ignorance.

"The Wise Man says, 'He who trusts in himself is a fool.'"

"This is spoken of an evil heart. But mine is good."

"How can you prove that?"

"It comforts me in the hope of heaven."

And thus they bantered back and forth, Christian answering each of Ignorance's assumptions with truth from the Bible.

"This faith of yours is nowhere in the Bible. True faith takes refuge in Christ's righteousness, not your own."

"What! Would you have us to trust what Christ has done without us? You would have us sin all we want, because we may be justified by Christ's personal righteousness as long as we believe in it?"

"Ignorance is your name, and so you are," said Christian. "You are ignorant of the true effects of faith in this righteousness of Christ, which is to commit your heart to God in Christ and to love His ways."

"Have you ever had Christ revealed to you

from heaven?" Hopeful asked Ignorance.

"What? You are a man for revelations! I believe that what both you and all the rest of you say about that matter is but the fruit of distracted brains."

"Why? Christ is so hid in God from the natural understanding of all flesh that He cannot by any man be known in salvation unless God the Father reveals Him to them."

"That is your faith, but not mine. I don't doubt mine is as good as yours," answered Ignorance.

"Give me leave to put in a word," Christian said. "You ought not to speak so lightly of this matter. I boldly affirm that no man can know Jesus Christ but by the revelation of the Father. Yes, and faith, too, by which the soul lays hold upon Christ, must be worked by the exceeding greatness of His mighty power. I perceive you are ignorant of the working of faith. So wake up, see your own wretchedness, and fly to the Lord Jesus. For by His righteousness, which is also the righteousness of God, you will be delivered from condemnation."

"I can't keep up with you," Ignorance said. "Go on ahead."

Christian and Hopeful chanted:

"Well, Ignorance, are you so foolish to

Reject good counsel, ten times given you?
And if you yet refuse it, you will know,
Too soon, the evil of your doing so.
Remember, man, in time: Yield. Do not fear.
Good counsel taken well saves; therefore hear.
But if you yet reject it, you will be
The loser, Ignorance, we guarantee."

"Come, Hopeful," Christian said. "I see that you and I must walk by ourselves again."

So they went on ahead as before, and Ignorance came hobbling after. Then Christian said, "I'm sorry for this poor man. It certainly will go badly for him at the end."

"Alas! There are an abundance in our town in his condition. Whole families, whole streets, pilgrims, too. And if there be that many in our parts, how many, do you think, must there be in the place where he was born?"

Moments later, Christian asked, "What do you think of such men? Do they have no conviction of sin, and as a consequence no fear of their dangerous condition?"

"Sometimes they may be fearful."

"And yet they don't know that such conviction of sin and consequent fear tend to their good. They try to stifle their fear. But 'The fear of the Lord is the beginning of wisdom.'"

"How do you describe right fear?" Hopeful asked.

"True or right fear is revealed in three things. First, it comes with a saving conviction of sin. Also, it drives the soul to lay hold of Christ for salvation. And finally, it births and continues in the soul as a great reverence of God, His Word, and His ways by keeping the soul tender and making it afraid to turn from these things to anything that would dishonor God, break its peace, grieve the Spirit, or cause the enemy to speak reproachfully."

"Well said. I believe you have the truth," Hopeful said. "Are we now almost past the Enchanted Ground?"

"Why?" Christian asked. "Are you weary of our discourse?"

"No, not at all. I just want to know where we are."

"We have about two miles farther to go. But let's return to our topic. Those who are ignorant of the things of God do not know that these convictions that tend to put them in fear are for their good, so they seek to stifle them."

"How?"

"They think that those fears are worked by the devil, and so they resist them as things they need to overthrow. They also think that these fears tend to spoil their faith, and they harden their hearts against them. They think they shouldn't fear, so they take on a false confidence. Then, too, they see that these fears take away their self-holiness, and so they resist them with all their might."

"I knew something of this myself. It was so with me before I knew myself."

"Well, let's leave our neighbor Ignorance by himself for now. Let's talk of something else. Did you know a man assertive in religion named Temporary?"

"Yes!" answered Hopeful. "He dwelt in Graceless, two miles from Honesty. He lived under the same roof as Turn-Back."

"Well, Temporary was awakened to his sins once. He even told me he was resolved to go on the pilgrimage. But after he grew acquainted with Save-Self, he became a stranger."

"He was a backslider," agreed Hopeful. "There were four reasons, I think. Although his conscience was awakened, his mind was unchanged. So when the power of guilt wore away, the things that provoked him to be religious faded away. So as his sense and fear of hell and damnation cooled, so his desires for heaven and salvation also cooled. And he was held by the world; he didn't want to lose everything, especially what others thought of him. He didn't want to bring unnecessary trouble his way. A third reason was the shame he felt for religion. Being proud and haughty doesn't go with religion, which is low and contemptible in his thinking. And lastly, he hated the feelings of guilt and hardened his heart. He chose ways to harden his heart more and more. And now you tell me how a man backslides."

"They block all thoughts of God, death, and judgment. Then by degrees they cast off their private duties of prayers, curbing their lusts, ogling, and guilt. They shun the company of Christians. They cast off public duties of hearing, reading, and conferring. Then they begin to make fun of the godly, so they feel better about leaving religion." Christian went on to describe the final slide into the company of evil men and carnal pleasures, first secretly, and finally openly.

Suddenly the two pilgrims realized the Enchanted Ground was behind them.

"Beulah Land!"

The air was sweet and pleasant, and their way lay directly through it. Here they heard continually the singing of birds, and saw every day new flowers appear in the earth. In this country the sun shone night and day because this was beyond the Valley of the Shadow of Death. It was also out of reach of Giant Despair. Here they were within sight of the City they were going to. Here they met some of the inhabitants of the country. The Shining Ones commonly walked in this land because it was on the borders of heaven. In this land the contract between the bride and the bridegroom was renewed. There was no want of corn and wine, for in this place they met with abundance of what they had sought in all their pilgrimage.

As they walked in this land, they had more rejoicing than in parts more remote from the Kingdom to which they were bound. And drawing near to the City, they had a more perfect view of it. It was built of pearls and precious stones. Also, the streets were paved with gold, so that by reason of the natural glory of the City and the reflection of the sunbeams upon it, Christian fell sick with desire to dwell there. Hopeful also had a bout or two of the same disease.

But being strengthened after a rest, they were better able to bear their sickness, and they walked on their way and came yet nearer and nearer. Orchards, vineyards, and gardens opened their gates onto the way. "Whose goodly vineyards and gardens are these?" called the pilgrims to a gardener standing in the way.

"They are the King's, planted here for His delight—and the solace of His pilgrims."

The gardener had them enter and invited them to refresh themselves. They ate delicacies and strolled the King's walks and arbors. And they slept. The pilgrims relaxed and took solace there for many days.

Finally the pilgrims no longer desired food or wine or sleep. They had to go on to the City. They could scarcely look at the City except through an instrument made for that purpose because the pure gold was so dazzlingly bright.

Two Shining Ones in golden robes met them. They asked the pilgrims where they came from. They also asked where they lodged along the way, what difficulties and danger they encountered, what comforts and pleasures they had met on the way. And the pilgrims answered all their questions.

Finally the Shining Ones said, "You have but two more difficulties and you are in the City."

Christian and Hopeful asked the men to go along with them.

"We will," they agreed. "But you must obtain it by your own faith."

So they went on together until they came within sight of the Gate.

Between them and the Celestial Gate was a river. There was no bridge, and the water was very deep. At the sight, the pilgrims were astounded, but the men with them said, "You must go through, or you cannot come to the Gate."

"Is there no other way to the Gate?" the pilgrims asked.

"Yes," the Shining Ones answered, "but only two, Enoch and Elijah, have been allowed to tread that path since the foundation of the world. And no one else will until the last trumpet sounds."

The pilgrims were despondent at this difficulty before them and tried to discover a way they could escape the river.

"Is the river all one depth?" asked Christian.

"You will find it deeper or shallower, as you believe in the King of the City," was the answer.

Then the pilgrims entered the water. Christian began to sink. He cried out to his good friend Hopeful, "The water is going over my head!"

"Be of good cheer, brother," said Hopeful. "I feel the bottom, and it is good."

"The sorrows of death have me, my friend. I shall not see the land that flows with milk and honey." Darkness and horror held Christian so that he could not see before him. In a great measure he lost his senses so that he could neither remember orderly talk nor any of the sweet refreshments he had met with along the way of his pilgrimage. He feared that he should die in that river and never obtain entrance at the Gate. Also he was troubled at the thought of the sins he had committed, both before and since he began his pilgrimage. He saw hobgoblins and evil spirits.

Hopeful had an awful time to keep his

brother's head above water. Sometimes Christian would completely sink under the water, and then arise above it half-dead.

"Brother, I see the Gate and men standing by to receive us," encouraged Hopeful.

"It is you they are waiting for. You were always hopeful. But for my sins He has brought me into this trap and left me."

"You have quite forgotten the Bible," said Hopeful. "The wicked 'have no struggles at their death. . . . They are free from burdens' carried by good men. The troubles that you have in these waters are no sign that God has forsaken you, but are sent to test you. Will you call to mind His goodness that you received before today? Be of good cheer. Jesus Christ will make you whole!"

"Oh, I see Him now! And He tells me, 'When you pass through the waters, I will be with you, and through the rivers, they shall not overflow thee,'" cried Christian.

Then they both took courage. After that the hobgoblins and evil spirits were as silent as stones. He felt bottom. The river was shallow.

When they reached the far bank of the river, they were met by the two Shining Ones. They said, "We are ministering spirits sent forth to those who shall be heirs to salvation."

So they went on toward the Gate. They sped

upward, though the foundation upon which the City was grounded was higher than the clouds. But the pilgrims went up the hill with ease because they had these two men to lead them up by the arms. They had left the mortal garments behind in the river. So they went up, sweetly talking as they went, being comforted because they safely crossed over the river and had such glorious companions to attend them.

The Shining Ones said, "You are going now to the paradise of God. You will see the Tree of Life and eat its imperishable fruit. You shall be given robes of light, and you will walk and talk every day with the King, for all eternity. You will see no sorrow, no sickness, no affliction, no death. These former things have passed away. You are going now to Abraham, Isaac, and Jacob, and to the prophets."

"But what must we do in the Holy Place?" asked Christian.

"You shall receive comfort for all your toil, and joy for all your sorrow. You reap what you have sown, even the fruit of your prayers and tears and sufferings for your King along the way. You must wear crowns of gold and enjoy the perpetual sight of the Holy One, for there you shall see Him as He is. There you shall serve Him continually with praise, with shouting, and with thanksgiving. Your eyes shall be delighted with seeing, and your ears with hearing the pleasant voice of the Mighty One. There you shall enjoy your friends again who have gone before you, and there you shall with joy receive even every one who follows into the Holy Place after you. When He shall come with sound of trumpet in the clouds, as upon wings of the wind, you shall come with Him. And when He sits upon the throne of judgment, you shall sit by Him. For whether it be angels or men, you shall have a voice in that judgment because they were His and your enemies. You will be forever with Him."

Now as they were drawing toward the Gate, a throng of Heavenly Hosts came out to surround them.

The two Shining Ones said, "These are the men who have loved our Lord when they were in the world, and they have left all for His Holy Name. He has sent us to fetch them and we have brought them this far on their journey."

The Heavenly Hosts gave a great shout and cried, "Blessed are those who are invited to the wedding supper of the Lamb! Blessed are they who do His commandments, that they may have the right to the Tree of Life, and may go through the Gate into the City."

Several of the King's trumpeters, clothed in white and shining raiment, made the heavens echo with their melodious and loud noises. They saluted Christian and Hopeful with ten thousand welcomes from the world.

After this, they surrounded the pilgrims and continually sounded the trumpets as they walked on together. Christian and his brother were amazed at the welcome they felt as more and more trumpeters joined the crowd around them. The pilgrims were swallowed up with the sight of angels and with the melodious notes. Now they had the City itself in view, and they thought they heard all the bells therein to ring in welcome. Thus they came to the Gate.

Over the Gate was written in letters of gold, "Blessed are they who do His commandments, that they may have right to the Tree of Life and may enter through the gates into the City."

After the Shining Ones instructed them, Christian and Hopeful cried to the Gate, "We call upon the Gatekeepers: Enoch, Moses, and Elijah."

Above the Gate three saints appeared. "What do you want?" they asked.

"These pilgrims come from the City of Destruction," cried the Shining Ones, "for the love they bear to the King of this place."

"Bring their certificates," commanded a voice from above.

Then the pilgrims handed the attendants the certificates that they had received in the beginning of their pilgrimage. The attendants carried the certificates to the King, who when He had read them said, "Where are these men?"

"They are standing without the Gate."

Then the same voice boomed through the heavens, "Open the Gate that the righteous may enter, those who keep faith!"

All the bells in the City rang again for joy. Christian and Hopeful entered, to be transfigured, crowned with glory, and adorned in garments that made them shine like the sun. Hovering were seraphim, cherubim, and creatures too dazzling to recognize. And the whole Heavenly Host cried, "Holy, Holy, Holy is the Lord God Almighty." And Christian and Hopeful joined them in immortality to gaze upon the Holy One.

After the Gate closed after the pilgrims, Ignorance came up to the river on the other side. But he soon got over, and without half the difficulty that the other two men met with. For it happened that there was then in that place one Vain-Hope, a ferryman, who with his boat helped him over. So Ignorance ascended the hill and came up to the Gate, alone. No one met him with the least encouragement. When he was come up to the Gate, he looked up to the writing that was above, and then began to knock, supposing that entrance should be quickly given to him.

But the men who looked over the top of the

Gate asked, "Where have you come from? And what do you want?"

He answered, "I have eaten and drunk in the presence of the King, and He has taught in our streets."

Then they asked him for his certificate that they might go in and show it to the King.

So he fumbled in his bosom for one and found none.

Then said they, "Do you have one?"

But the man answered never a word.

So they told the King, but He would not come down to see him but commanded the two Shining Ones, who conducted Christian and Hopeful to the City, to go out and take Ignorance and bind him hand and foot and have him away.

Then they took him up and carried him through the air to the door in the side of the hill and put him in there. It was a way to hell, even from the gates of Heaven.

෨

Meanwhile, back in the City of Destruction, Christian's wife was in torment. Losing her husband had cost her many a tear. She remembered his restless groans, his tears, his burden. After Christian went over the river and she could hear of him no more, her thoughts began to work in her mind.

She considered herself and whether her unbecoming behavior toward her husband was one reason she saw her husband no more. And that because of her he was taken away. Then came into her mind, by swarms, all her unkind, unnatural, and ungodly behavior toward her friends. These clogged her conscience and loaded her with guilt. She remembered how she hardened her heart against all his entreaties and loving persuasions he used with both her and their sons to go with him. All Christian said or did assaulted her memory and ripped her heart in two. His bitter cry, "What shall I do to be saved?" rang in her ears.

Finally she said to her four boys, "Sons, I have sinned against your father. I would not go with him, and I have robbed you of everlasting life."

Then the boys all fell into tears and cried out to go after their father.

"Oh," said the woman, "if only we had gone with your father. Then it would have been well with us. But now it is likely to be a very difficult journey without him. Even though I foolishly thought that your father's troubles proceeded from a silly fancy he had, or that he was overtaken with depression, yet now I cannot get them out of my mind. Now I believe they sprang from another cause—the light of eternal life was given him. And with that light's help he has escaped the snares of death."

Then they all wept again.

That night she dreamed. A parchment was unrolled before her, in which was recorded all her ways, and they were black indeed. She cried out, "Lord, have mercy on me, a sinner." And her children heard her.

Almost immediately, two foul-looking creatures were beside her bed, saying, "What shall we do with this woman? If she continues this, we will lose her as surely as we lost her husband. We must by one way or another seek to take her off from the thoughts of what should be after this life, else all the world cannot stop her from becoming a pilgrim."

Next morning she awoke in a great sweat, and she started to tremble. But after a while she fell asleep again. When she dreamed this time, she saw Christian, her husband, in a place of bliss among many immortals. He had a harp in his hand, and he stood and played it before One who sat on a throne with a rainbow about His head. She also saw Christian bow his head, placing his face on the pavement under the Prince's feet, saying, "I heartily thank my Lord and King for bringing me into this place." Then shouted a company of them who stood round about and harped. But no living man could tell what they said.

Later, she got up, prayed to God, and talked with her children awhile. When there was a hard knock on the door, she called, "If you come in God's name, come in."

A man answered, "Amen." He opened the door and greeted her: "Peace be to this house. Do you know why I come?"

Then she blushed and trembled, and her heart grew warm with desire to know where he came from and what his business was with her.

"My name is Secret. I dwell with those on high. They tell me you are now aware of your sin done to your husband when you hardened your heart to his way and in keeping your children in ignorance. Also, that you have a desire to go to the place where I live. The Merciful One has sent me to tell you that He is a God ready to forgive, and that He takes delight the more pardons He gives. He invites you to come into His presence, to His table, and He will feed you with the fat of His house and with the heritage of your father.

"Christian, your husband, is there with legions more of his companions. They always behold the face that ministers life to the beholders. And they will all be glad when they hear the sound of your feet step over your Father's threshold."

The woman was disconcerted and embarrassed. She bowed her head to the ground.

The visitor continued to speak. "Here is a letter for you from the King."

She took it and opened a perfumed letter. Letters of gold read: "I want you to come as your husband did on the way to the Celestial City, and dwell in My presence with joy forever."

"Oh, sir," she cried, quite overcome. "Won't you carry me and the boys with you, so that we may worship the King?"

"The bitter comes before the sweet," he answered. "You must go through troubles, as he did who went before you, before you enter the Celestial City. I advise you to do as Christian did. Go to the wicket gate over beyond the plain, for that is the entrance to the way you should go. Keep the letter with you. Read it often to yourself and to your children until you have learned it by heart. It is one of the songs that you must sing while you are in this house of your pilgrimage. You must deliver it at the Celestial Gate."

Then she called the boys. "My sons, I have been under much stress in my soul about the death of your father; not that I doubt at all of his happiness, for I am satisfied now that he is well. I have also been much affected with the thoughts of my own state and yours, which is miserable by nature. My behavior to your father in his distress is a great load to my conscience, for I hardened both my own heart and yours against him and refused to go with him on pilgrimage.

"The thoughts of these things would now

kill me outright but for a dream which I had last night and for the encouragement that Secret has given me this morning. Come, my children, let us pack up and be gone to the gate that leads to the Celestial City, that we may see your father and be with him and his companions in peace, according to the laws of that land."

The boys burst into tears of joy. Secret then left, and they began to prepare for their journey.

Soon there was another knock on the door.

"If you come in God's name, come in," answered the wife of Christian, who now called herself Christiana.

Two stunned neighbors entered: Mrs. Timorous and the maiden Mercy. They were unused to hearing this kind of language from Christiana.

"Why are you packing?" asked Mrs. Timorous.

"I am preparing for a journey," Christiana answered.

"What journey?"

"To follow my good husband." Christiana burst into tears.

"Oh, I hope this isn't true, good neighbor. For your children's sake, don't cast yourself away."

"They are going with me. Not one of them is willing to be left behind." Christiana went on to tell her everything, even reading the letter from the messenger.

"Oh, the madness that possesses you and your husband to run yourselves upon such difficulties," replied Mrs. Timorous. "You have heard, I am sure, what your husband did meet with, even in a manner at the first step that he took on his way. We also heard how he met with the lions, Apollyon, the Shadow of Death, and many other things. Nor can you forget the danger that he met with at Vanity Fair. For a man, he was so hard put to it, what can you, being but a poor woman, do? Have you even considered that you are not only being so rash as to cast yourself away, but you are planning to do it to your children as well? If for nothing else, stay home for the sake of your sweet children."

"Don't tempt me, my neighbor," said Christiana. "I have now a price put into my hand to get gain, and I should be a fool of the greatest size if I should have no heart to strike in with the opportunity. And for all these troubles you speak of that I am likely to meet in the way, they are so far off from being to me a discouragement that they show I am in the right. The bitter comes before the sweet and makes the sweet even sweeter. Please leave. You did not come here in God's name. I don't need you to disturb me further."

"Come on, Mercy!" snapped Mrs. Timorous. "This fool scorns our counsel."

But Mercy said, "Since this is Christiana's

farewell, I will walk a little way with her."

Mrs. Timorous said, "I suspect you are thinking of going with her. Well, take heed: We are out of danger here in the City of Destruction. I can't wait to talk to Mrs. Bats-Eyes, Mrs. Inconsiderate, Mrs. Light-Mind, and Mrs. Know-Nothing. They know I'm right."

Christiana and the boys were soon on the way, and Mercy went along with her.

Christiana said, "Mercy, I take this as an unexpected favor, that you should set foot out of doors with me, to accompany me a little in my way."

Then young Mercy said, "If I thought it would be to a good purpose to go with you, I would never go near the town anymore."

Christiana said, "Cast your lot with us, Mercy. I know well what will be the end of our pilgrimage. For I am sure not all the gold in Spain could make my husband sorry he is there in that place. You won't be rejected, even if you go along with me as my servant. We will have all things in common between us if only you go along with me."

"But how do I know that? If I had this hope from one who could tell, I would make no stick at all, but would go, though the way was never so tedious."

"Well, loving Mercy, I will tell you what you shall do. Come with me to the wicket gate. There

I will inquire further for you. See if you are allowed to enter. If you aren't given encouragement to continue, then I will be content to let you return to your house. I will also pay you for your kindness you've shown to me and my children in accompanying us in our way as you're doing."

"Then I will go that far with you and will take what shall follow. Lord, grant that my lot will fall with you," prayed Mercy.

Christiana was glad in her heart that not only did she have a companion, but she had prevailed with this poor maiden to fall in love with her own salvation.

As they went along, Mercy began weeping. "My poor relatives remain in our sinful town, and there is no one to encourage them to come."

"Your leaving will encourage them, just as Christian's encouraged me. The Lord gathers our tears and puts them into His bottle. These tears of yours, Mercy, will not be lost. For the Truth has said that they who sow in tears shall reap in joy and singing, bearing precious seed. And they shall doubtless come again with rejoicing, bringing his sheaves with him."

Then Mercy said:

"Let the Most Blessed be my guide,
If 't be His blessed will,
Into His gate, into His fold,

Up to His Holy Hill.
And let Him gather those of mine
Whom I have left behind."

❧

When they came to the Slough of Despond, Christiana stopped. "This is the place in which my dear husband was nearly smothered with mud." She also saw that in spite of the King's command to make this place good for pilgrims, it was worse than before.

But Mercy said, "Come, let us venture in, only let us be careful."

So they did not plunge straight in but found the steps.

As soon as they had crossed the slough, they heard someone speaking. He said, "Blessed is she that believes, for there shall be a performance of the things that have been told her from the Lord."

As they went on again, Mercy said to Christiana, "Had I a good reason to hope for a loving reception at the wicket gate as you, I think no Slough of Despond would discourage me."

"You know your affliction and I know mine, and, good friend, we shall all have enough evil before we come to our journey's end. For it can be imagined that the people who desire to attain such excellent glories as we do and who are so envied the happiness we have can expect to meet with what fears and scares, troubles and afflictions those who hate us can possibly assault us with."

Soon Christiana, Mercy, and the boys approached the wicket gate. They had a discussion as to how to approach the gate and what should be said to the gatekeeper. Then Christiana, since she was the oldest, knocked on the gate. She knocked and knocked, but no one answered.

Then they heard a dog barking at them. It sounded like a very large dog, and it made the women and children afraid to knock anymore for fear the mastiff should fly at them. Now they weren't sure what to do. They didn't want to knock for fear of the dog. Nor did they want to turn away, in case the gatekeeper did finally come to the gate and be offended with them for knocking and walking away.

Just as they were thinking of knocking again, the gatekeeper said, "Who is there?"

The dog quit barking, and the gatekeeper opened the narrow gate.

Christiana bowed low before the gatekeeper and said, "Let not our lord be offended with his handmaidens because we have knocked at his princely gate."

"Where do you come from? What do you want?" he asked.

Christiana said, "We come from the same

place Christian came from, and we're on the same errand as he. We want to be admitted through this gate to the way that leads to the Celestial City. I am Christiana, the wife of Christian, who is now gone above."

"What?" marveled the keeper. "Are you now a pilgrim, who once despised that life?"

She bowed her head and said, "Yes, and these are my sweet children also."

He waved her in and the boys, too, saying, "Let the little children come to me." A trumpet sounded for joy, and the gatekeeper shut the gate.

All this time, Mercy stood outside the gate, trembling and crying for fear that she was rejected. But when Christiana gained admittance for herself and her boys, then she made intercession for Mercy. "My lord, I have a companion of mine who is still standing outside the gate. She has come for the same reason as myself. She is dejected because she thinks that without the King sending for her, she cannot come in."

Just then Mercy came to the end of her patience, for each minute felt like a hour that she waited for Christiana to intercede for her. So she knocked at the gate herself. And she knocked so loud that Christiana started. "It is my friend," she told the gatekeeper.

So the gatekeeper reopened the gate and

looked out. But Mercy had fainted with fear that no gate would be opened to her.

Then the gatekeeper took her by the hand and said, "Girl, I bid you arise."

"Oh, sir," she said. "I am faint. There is scarcely any life left in me."

But the gatekeeper said, "Don't be afraid. Stand up and tell me why you have come."

Mercy blurted, "I am come even though I was never invited as my friend Christiana was. Hers was from the King, and mine is from her. But I fear to presume."

"Did she desire that you come with her to this place?"

"Yes, and as you see I have come. If there is any grace and forgiveness of sins to spare, please let me in, too."

Then he took her by the hand and gently led her in. "I take all who believe in to me, by whatever means they come to me." Then he called on his servants to bring a bundle of myrrh for Mercy to smell in order to stop her fainting.

Inside, all six pilgrims said they were sorry for their sins and begged his forgiveness. He granted them pardon and told them that along the way they would see what deed saved them. He continued to speak words of comfort and gladness to them, and they were greatly encouraged.

So he left them for a while in a summer

parlor where they talked by themselves.

Christiana spoke first. "How glad I am that we are here!"

"So well you may, but I of all of us have reason to leap for joy," Mercy said.

"I did think as I stood outside the gate that all our work was for nothing, especially when that dog made such a heavy barking against us."

"My worst fear was after you and the boys were taken into the gatekeeper's favor and I was left behind. I thought the scripture was fulfilled when it says, 'Two women shall be grinding together; the one shall be taken, and the other left.' It was all I could do to keep from crying out, 'Undone! Undone!' I was so afraid to knock anymore, but when I looked up to what was written over the gate, I took courage. It was either knock again or die. So I knocked. But I'm not sure how, because my spirit then struggled between life and death.

"I was in such a state! The door was shut on me, and there was a most terrible dog somewhere about. Who wouldn't have knocked as I did with all their might? Tell me, what said my lord about my rudeness? Wasn't he angry with me?"

"I believe what you did pleased him well enough, for he showed no sign to the contrary. But I am surprised that he keeps such a dog. If I'd known that, I'm afraid I may have not had the heart to venture forth. But now we are in, and I am glad with all my heart."

"I will ask the gatekeeper why he keeps such a dog the next time we see him. I hope he won't take it wrong."

"Yes, do ask," said the children. "We are afraid he will bite us when we leave this place."

At last the gatekeeper came down to them again. Mercy fell to the ground on her face before him and worshipped and said, "Let my lord accept the sacrifice of praise which I now offer unto him with my lips."

He said to her, "Be at peace and stand up."

"Why do you keep such a cruel dog?" asked Mercy, still shaken.

"He belongs to Beelzebub, to frighten pilgrims from the way. He has frightened many honest pilgrims. But there is nothing I can do. He hopes to keep pilgrims from knocking at the gate for entrance. Sometimes the dog has broken out and scared those I love. But I take it all patiently. I also give my pilgrims timely help so they are not delivered up to his power to do whatever his doggish nature would prompt him to."

Then Mercy said, "I confess my ignorance. I spoke of what I didn't understand. You do all things well. I should have known better."

Then Christiana began to speak of the journey and to inquire after the way. So the gatekeeper fed them, washed their feet, and set them in the way of his steps, much the same as he dealt with Christian.

So the pilgrims went on the way, between the walls of salvation. Suddenly Christiana saw the two foul-looking creatures she had seen in her dream. They came toward her as if to embrace her.

"Stand back or pass peaceably," she warned them.

But they didn't listen and tried to lay hands on the women. But Christiana, very angry now, kicked at them. Mercy also followed Christiana's example.

Again Christiana spoke to them: "Stand back and be gone. We have no money to lose since we are pilgrims."

"We don't want your money. If you will grant one small request that we ask, we will make women of you forever," they replied and tried to embrace Christiana and Mercy. But they tried again to walk around the men. But they blocked the way against Christiana and Mercy.

"You would have us body and soul. I know this is why you have come. But we would rather die on the spot than suffer ourselves to be brought into such snares that will harm our well-being forever." Then both Christiana and Mercy screamed, "Murder! Murder!" But the men still would not leave the women alone. So they cried out again.

Several in the gatekeeper's house heard the screams and came to investigate. They found the women in a great scuffle with the men while the children looked on crying.

"Would you make my lord's people sin?" demanded one of the men who appeared on the way.

The man attempted to take the other men, but the two fiends jumped the wall and escaped into the realm of Beelzebub. They were seen joining the cruel mastiff.

"I marveled when you came in the gate that you did not ask our lord for a protector," said the man. "He would have granted you one."

"We felt so blessed by present blessing we forgot all future danger," said Christiana. "Should we go back and ask for one?"

"No. Go ahead. I will tell him of your confession. But remember: 'Ask and it will be given to you.'" And the man went back to the gate.

Mercy said, "I thought we were past all danger and that we should never sorrow again. What happened?"

"I am to blame," said Christiana. "I was warned in a dream these two fiends would try to prevent my salvation."

"Well, we have had a chance to see our imperfections. And the Lord has taken the occasion to reveal the riches of His grace. He has delivered us from the hands of those who were stronger than us."

When they had talked away a little more time, they came near a house by the way. As they came closer, they heard a lot of talking within the house, and thought they heard Christiana's name spoken.

Word of Christiana's pilgrimage with her children went before them. It was pleasing news, especially to those who knew she was Christian's wife.

So they stood at the door and listened to the talk within. Finally, Christiana knocked on the door.

A maiden opened the door. "To whom do you wish to speak?"

"We understand this is a privileged place for pilgrims. I am Christiana, the wife of Christian, who some time ago traveled this way. These are his four children. The maiden is my companion and is also going on pilgrimage. We pray that there is room for us, for the day is nearly over, and we don't wish to continue any farther at night."

The maiden ran inside, yelling, "Christiana and her children are at the door!" The pilgrims heard rejoicing inside the house. Soon the master, the Interpreter, came to the door. "Come in, daughter of Abraham. Come, boys. Come, maiden Mercy."

So when they were within, they were bidden to sit down and rest. Those who had attended Christian came into the room to see his family. They all smiled for joy because Christiana had become a pilgrim.

After a while, because supper wasn't ready, the Interpreter took them into his significant rooms. Soon they saw all the things Christian had seen: the picture of Christ, the devil trying to extinguish grace, the man in the cage, and the rest.

Then the Interpreter took them into another room. There was a man who could look no way but down. He held a rake in his hand. One stood over the man's head with a celestial crown in his hand. He offered to give him the crown for his rake, but the man neither looked up nor acknowledged the other man. Instead he raked the straws, the small sticks, and dust on the floor toward him.

"Is this the figure of the man of the world?" asked Christiana.

"Yes," said the Interpreter. "The rake is his carnal mind. He is so intent on raking straw and dust and sticks he doesn't see God. Heaven is but a fable to some, and the things of this earth are the only substantial things. The man can only look down. It is to show that when earthly things control a man's mind, his heart is carried away from God."

Then they went into a sumptuous room.

"What do you see here? Anything profitable?" asked the Interpreter.

Christiana was quick to see a large spider on the wall. But Mercy saw nothing. The Interpreter told Mercy to look again. "There is nothing here but a big, ugly spider who hangs on the wall."

"Is there but one spider in all this spacious room?"

Then the water stood in Christiana's eye. "This shows how the ugliest creatures full of the venom of sin belong in the King's house. God has made nothing in vain."

"You have said the truth," Interpreter said to her. This made Mercy blush, and the boys covered their faces, for they all began to understand the riddle.

He then took them into another room where a hen and her chickens were. One of the chickens went to the trough to drink, and every time she drank, she lifted up her head and her eyes toward heaven. "See what this little chick does," said the Interpreter. "Learn of her to acknowledge from where your mercies come, by receiving them with looking up."

As they watched more, they saw that the hen walked in a fourfold method toward her chickens. She had a common call, a special call she only used sometimes, a brooding note, and an outcry.

"Now compare this hen to your King and the chickens to His obedient ones. The King walks toward His people with His common call in which He gives nothing, his special call with which He always has something to give, His brooding voice for those under His wing, and an outcry to give the alarm when He sees the enemy coming."

The Interpreter went on to show them more riddles, and then he gave them one wise saying after another. "The fatter the sow is, the more she desires the mire; the fatter the ox is, the more gamesomely he goes to the slaughter; and the more healthy the lusty man is, the more prone he is to evil. There is a desire in women to go neat and fine, and it is a comely thing to be adorned with that. That in God's sight is of great price."

When he was done with the wise sayings, the Interpreter took them out into his garden and showed them a tree whose inside was all rotten and gone. Yet it grew and had leaves.

Mercy asked, "What does this mean?"

"This tree whose outside is fair and whose inside is rotten is to which many people could be compared who are in God's garden. With their mouths they speak high in behalf of God, but indeed will do nothing for Him. Their leaves are fair, but their heart is good for nothing but to be tinder for the devil's tinderbox."

Now supper was ready, the table spread, and all things set on the board. So they sat down and did eat after one had given thanks. It was the Interpreter's custom to entertain those who lodged with him with music at meals. So the minstrels played. One who sang had a very fine voice. His song was like this:

"The Lord is only my support,
And He that doth me feed;
How can I then want anything
Whereof I stand in need?"

After the music, the Interpreter asked Christiana and Mercy to tell him of their reasons for starting the pilgrimage. Though each had a different story to tell, he commended them for their good start and for already showing courage along the way. Later, Mercy could not sleep for the joy the Interpreter's words to her had inspired. At last her doubts were gone, so she lay blessing and praising God who had such favor for her.

In the morning they arose with the sun and bathed. They came out not only sweet and clean, but enlivened and strengthened. They donned fine linen, white and clean. The Interpreter called for his seal and marked their faces, so they looked like angels. And each accused the other of being fairer because they could not see their own glory.

Then the Interpreter called for a manservant of his. A huge man appeared.

The Interpreter said, "Take your sword, helmet, and shield, Great-Heart, and escort these pilgrims to the Palace Beautiful." And to the pilgrims he said, "Godspeed."

The pilgrims departed, singing:

> *"This place has been a pleasant stage,*
> *Here we have heard and eyed*
> *Those good things that are age to age*
> *Hid from the evil side."*

∾

Great-Heart went before them. They soon came to the Cross, where Christian's burden had tumbled into the sepulcher. Here they made a pause, and here they blessed God.

Christiana said, "Now I remember the gatekeeper told us we would come to the word and deed by which we are pardoned. By word which is by the promise, and by deed, which was in the way our pardon was obtained. I know something of the promise, but of the deed and how it should be obtained, I don't know. Mr. Great-Heart, if you know, please, let us hear your discourse thereof."

"We are redeemed from sin at a price," said Great-Heart. "And that price was the blood of your Lord, who came and stood in your place. He has performed righteousness to cover you and the spilt blood to wash you in."

"But if He parts with His righteousness to us, what will He have for Himself?"

"He has more righteousness than you have need of, or than He needs Himself."

"Now I see that there was something to be learned by our being pardoned by word and deed. Good Mercy, let us labor to keep this in mind. And, my children, you remember it also. But, sir, was not this that made my good Christian's burden fall from off his shoulder and that made him give three leaps for joy?"

"Yes, it was the belief of this that cut out those strings that could not be cut by other means."

"My heart is ten times lighter and more joyous now," said Christiana, "yet it makes my heart ache to think He bled for me."

"There is not only comfort and ease of a burden brought to us by the sight and consideration of these things, but an endeared affection that is born in us by it. For who can but be affected with the way and means of redemption and so with the Man who worked it for him?"

"It makes my heart bleed to think that He should bleed for me," said Christiana. "You deserve to have me: You have bought me. You deserve to have me all, for You have paid for me ten thousand times more than I am worth."

"You speak now in the warmth of your affection," said Great-Heart. "I hope you always will be able to."

They went on until they came to the place where Simple, Sloth, and Presumption lay and slept when Christian went by. Now they came upon the three men hanging by the way in irons.

"Who are these men?" asked Mercy. "What did they do?"

Great-Heart answered, "They are Simple, Sloth, and Presumption. They had no intention to be pilgrims but only to hinder the pilgrims who passed by. They turned several out of the way: Slow-Pace, Short-Wind, No-Heart, Linger-after-Lust, Sleepy-Head, and Dull."

Christiana said, "They got just what they deserved, then."

After that they came to the foot of the Hill of Difficulty. The spring where Christian refreshed himself, which was once so pure, was now muddy. Great-Heart explained, "The evil ones do not want pilgrims to quench their thirst. Put it in a vessel and let the dirt settle. It will be pure again."

The two byways, Destruction and Danger, had been barred by chains. "'The way of the sluggard is blocked. . .but the path of the upright is a highway,'" quoted Christiana of the wise man Solomon.

"Yet some pilgrims still take the byways," said Great-Heart, "because the hill is very hard."

So they went forward and began to go up the hill. Before they reached the top, Christiana began to pant and said, "I daresay, this is a breathing hill. No marvel if they who love their ease more than their souls choose for themselves a smoother way."

Then said Mercy, "I must sit down."

Then the smallest child began to cry.

"Come, come," said Great-Heart, "don't sit down here. A little bit farther on is the Prince's arbor." Then he took the boy by the hand and led him up to the arbor.

When they came to the arbor, they were all willing to sit down and rest because of the pelting heat.

Mercy said, "How good is the Prince of pilgrims to provide such resting places for them! I have heard much of this arbor. Let's beware of sleeping, for as I have heard it cost poor Christian dearly."

As they rested, Christiana set out food to refresh their bodies. After a while, Great-Heart said,

"The day is wearing away. If you think good, let us prepare to get going." So they got up to go.

But Christiana forgot to take her bottle of spirits with her, so she sent one of the boys back to fetch it.

Then Mercy said, "I think this is a losing place. Here Christian lost his roll, and here Christiana left her bottle behind her. Sir, what is the cause of this?"

"The cause is sleep or forgetfulness. Some sleep when they should keep awake, and some forget when they should remember. And this is the reason why often at the resting places, some pilgrims come off losers. Pilgrims should watch and remember what they have already received under their greatest enjoyments. But because they don't do so, many times their rejoicing ends in tears and their sunshine in a cloud."

After they topped the Hill, Great-Heart gathered them beside him to walk between the lions. The boys, instead of leading the way as they had done, lined up behind Great-Heart. He drew his sword with the intent to make a way for the pilgrims in spite of the lions.

Suddenly a giant appeared beyond the lions. He called out to Great-Heart, "Guide, what is the cause of your coming here?"

Great-Heart called, "These are pilgrims, and this is the way they must go."

"I am Grim. Some call me Bloody-Man. This is no longer the way."

"I see now the path is overgrown with grass," said Great-Heart angrily. "You must be stopping pilgrims." He lunged at Grim with his sword. "This is the King's highway, and these women and children will follow it."

His sword came down on the giant's helmet and brought him down. The giant writhed on the ground, dying.

When the giant was dead, Great-Heart said to the pilgrims, "Come now, and follow me. No hurt shall happen to you from the lions."

They therefore went on, but the women trembled as they passed by the lions. The boys also looked as if they would die, but they all got by without further hurt.

It was getting dark, so they made haste to the porter's gate. Soon Great-Heart knocked on the gate to a palace. He had only to say, "Porter, it is I," and the gate opened. But the porter did not see the women and children standing behind Great-Heart.

The porter asked, "What is your business here so late tonight, Great-Heart?"

"I have brought some pilgrims here, where by my lord's commandment they must lodge. I would have been here sooner if I had not been opposed by the giant who used to back the lions. But after a

163

long and tedious combat with him, I have cut him off and have brought the pilgrims here to safety."

"Will you not go in and stay till morning?"

"No, I will return to my lord tonight."

Then the pilgrims realized Great-Heart was going back to the Interpreter's house. They begged him to stay. "I know not how to be willing you should leave us in our pilgrimage. You have been so faithful and so loving to us. You have fought so stoutly for us. You have been so hearty in counseling us that I shall never forget your favor toward us," Christiana said.

Mercy said, "Oh that we might have your company to our journey's end! How can such poor women as we hold out in a way so full of troubles as this way is without friend or defender?"

"I am at my lord's command," he replied. "You should have asked him to let me go all the way with you. He would have granted your request. For now, I must return. Good-bye."

Then the porter, Mr. Watchful, asked Christiana of her country and kindred. She told him she came from the City of Destruction. "I am a widow. My husband is dead. His name was Christian."

The porter then rang the bell. A maiden answered the door to the palace. Upon learning Christiana was the wife of Christian, she rushed back inside where there followed the sound of rejoicing. The pilgrims received a great welcome. They met Prudence, Piety, and Charity. They feasted on lamb and ended supper with a prayer and a psalm. Christiana asked to spend the night in the same room where her husband had slept.

"Little did I think once," said Christiana, "that I should ever follow my husband, much less worship the Lord with him."

Next morning the pilgrims sent a message back to the Interpreter's house requesting Great-Heart for their escort on the rest of the journey.

After about a week at the palace, Mercy had a visitor who pretended some goodwill to her. His name was Mr. Brisk, a man of some breeding who pretended to religion, but a man who stuck very close to the world. So he came once or twice or more to Mercy and offered love to her. Now Mercy had a fair countenance and was very alluring.

Her mind also was always busying herself in doing, from when she had nothing to do for herself, she would make hose and garments for others and would give them to others as had need. Mr. Brisk, not knowing where or how she disposed of what she made, seemed to be greatly taken, for he never found her idle. He thought she would be a good housewife.

Mercy then revealed the business to the maidens of the household and inquired of them concerning Mr. Brisk, for they knew him better than she. So they told her that he was a very busy young man, one who pretended to religion, but was really a stranger to the power of that which is good.

"No, I will look no more on him," said Mercy. "For I have purposed never to have a clog to my soul."

Prudence then replied, "You don't need a great matter of discouragement. Just continue doing as you have for the poor. That will quickly cool his courage."

So the next time he came, he found her at her work, making things for the poor.

"What, always at it?" he asked.

"Yes," she said, "either for myself or for others."

"What do you earn in a day?"

"I do these things that I may be rich in good work, laying up in store a good foundation against the time to come that I may lay hold on eternal life."

"What do you do with them?"

"Clothe the naked," she said.

His countenance fell. And he didn't come to see her again. When asked as to the reason why, he said that Mercy was a pretty lass but troubled with ill conditions.

After a month had passed, the family where Christiana was saw that they had a purpose to go forward. They called the whole house together to give thanks to their King for sending them such profitable guests as these.

Then they said to Christiana, "We shall show you something that we do to all pilgrims. It is something you can meditate on when you are on the way."

So they took Christiana, her children, and Mercy into the closet and showed them one of the apples that Eve did eat of and then gave to her husband. They asked Christiana what she thought the object was.

Christiana said, "Food or poison. I don't know which."

So they opened the matter to her, and she held up her hands and wondered.

Then they took her to a place and showed her Jacob's ladder. They watched the angels ascending and descending while they watched. They saw many other things their hosts wanted to show them.

Finally Great-Heart arrived. And when the porter opened the door and let him in, what joy there was at being reunited with their friend.

Then said Great-Heart to Christiana and to Mercy, "My lord has sent each of you a bottle of wine, and also some parched corn, together with a couple of pomegranates. He has also sent the boys some figs and raisins to refresh you in your way."

Then they put their attention to their journey, and Prudence and Piety went along with them. When they came to the gate, Christiana asked the porter if anyone came by lately.

"No, the only one was awhile ago, but he told me that there had been a great robbery committed on the King's highway as you go. But he said the thieves were taken and will shortly be tried for their lives."

Christiana and Mercy were afraid until Matthew reminded them of Great-Heart. So the little group left the palace and went forward to the brow of the hill. Piety then remembered something she'd planned to give to Christiana and her companions. So she went back to get it. While she was gone, Christiana thought she heard in a grove a little way off on the right hand a very curious melodious note.

Christiana asked Prudence about the one making the curious notes. "They are our country birds. I often keep them tame in our house. They are very fine for company when we are melancholy. They make the woods and groves and solitary places desirable to be in."

By this time Piety had returned. So she said

to Christiana, "Look here, I have brought you a scheme of all those things that you saw at our house. You may look on this when you find yourself forgetful and call those things again to remembrance for your edification and comfort."

Then the pilgrims descended into the Valley of Humiliation. It was steep and slippery, but they were careful, so they got down pretty well.

"This valley is a most fruitful place," reassured Great-Heart. "See how green the valley. See how beautiful the lilies. Listen to the shepherd boy over there."

The pilgrims heard the boy sing:

"He who is down, need fear no fall;
He who is low, no pride.
He who is humble, ever shall
Have God to be his guide.
I am content with what I have,
Be it little or much:
And, Lord, yet more content I crave,
because You save such.
Fullness to those, is all a blight,
Who go on pilgrimage:
Here little, and after delight,
Is best from age to age."

Great-Heart went on to tell of the features of

the valley. "Did I say our Lord had his country house here in former days? He loved to walk here. To the people who live here, He has left a yearly revenue to be faithfully paid them at certain seasons for their maintenance and for their further encouragement to go on their pilgrimage."

Soon the pilgrims came to a pillar that read:

Let Christian's slips, before he came here, and the battles he met with in this place, be a warning to those who come after.

"Forgetful Green here is the most dangerous place in all these parts," explained Great-Heart. "This is where pilgrims have trouble if they forget favors they have received and how unworthy they are. This is where Christian fought Apollyon. Christian's blood is on the stones to this day. Look. There are Apollyon's broken arrows. When Apollyon was beaten, he retreated into the next valley, which is called the Valley of the Shadow of Death."

As they entered the Valley of the Shadow of Death, they heard groaning, as if from great torment. The ground shook and hissed. A fiend approached them, then vanished.

" 'Resist the devil, and he shall flee from you,' " remembered one of the pilgrims.

They heard a great padding beast behind them. Its every roar made the valley echo. When Great-Heart turned to face it, it too vanished. Then a great mist and darkness fell, so that they could not see. They heard the noise and rustling of the enemies.

"Many have spoken of the Valley of the Shadow of Death," said Christiana, "but no one can know what it means until they come into it themselves. 'Each heart knows its own bitterness, and no one can share its joy.' To be here is a fearful thing."

Great-Heart added, "This is like doing business in great waters, or like going down into the deep. This is like being in the heart of the sea, and like going down to the bottoms of the mountains. Now it seems as if the earth, with its bars, surrounds us forever. But let them who walk in darkness, and have no light, trust in the name of the Lord, and stay upon their God. For my part, as I have told you already, I have gone often through this valley, and have been much harder put to it than now I am; and yet you see I am alive. I would not boast, for that I am not my own savior. But I trust we shall have a good deliverance. Come, let us pray for light to Him who can rebuke all the devils in hell."

So they cried and prayed, and God sent light and deliverance, for there was now no obstruction in their way. Then they were stopped with a pit. Yet they were not through the valley, so they went on still, and behold great stinks and loathsome smells, to the great annoyance of them. Then said Mercy to Christiana, "It is not so pleasant being here as at the gate, or at the Interpreter's, or at the house where we lay last."

"Oh but," said one of the boys, "it is not so bad to go through here, as it is to abide here always. For all I know, one reason why we must go this way to the House prepared for us is that our home might be made the sweeter to us."

"Well said, Samuel," said the Guide. "You have now spoken like a man."

"Why, if ever I get out here again," said the boy, "I think I shall prize light and good way better than ever I did in all my life."

Then said the Guide, "We shall be out by and by."

So on they went, and Joseph said, "Can't we see to the end of this valley yet?"

Then said the Guide, "Look to your feet, for you shall presently be among snares." So they looked to their feet and went on, but they were troubled much with the snares. Now when they had come among the snares, they saw a man cast into the ditch on the left hand, with his flesh all rent and torn.

Then said the Guide, "That is one Heedless,

who was going this way. He has lain there a great while. There was one Take-Heed with him, when he was taken and slain; but he escaped their hands. You cannot imagine how many are killed hereabouts, and yet men are so foolishly venturous as to set out lightly on pilgrimage, and to come without a guide. Poor Christian! It was a wonder that he here escaped. But he was beloved of his God. Also he had a good heart of his own, or else he could never have done it."

They continued on. Ahead of them was an old man. They knew he was a pilgrim by his staff and his clothes. The old man turned defensively.

"I am a guide for these pilgrims to the Celestial City," explained Great-Heart.

"I beg your pardon. I was afraid you were of those who robbed Little-Faith some time ago."

"And what could you have done if we had been of that company?" puzzled Great-Heart.

"Why, I would have fought so hard I'm sure you couldn't have given me the best of it. No Christian can be overcome unless he gives up himself."

"Well said," marveled Great-Heart. "What is your name?"

"My name is Honest. I only wish that was my nature." When Honest learned who the pilgrims were, he gushed to Christiana, "I have heard of your husband. His name rings all over these parts of the world for his faith, his courage, his endurance, and his sincerity."

As they walked, Honest and Great-Heart discussed a pilgrim whom they both knew: Fearing.

"What could be the reason that such a good man should be so much in the dark?" asked Honest.

"The wise God will have it so. Some must pipe, and some must weep. Though the notes of the bass are woeful, some say it is the ground of music."

As they continued on their way, they found a giant holding a man, rifling his pockets. Great-Heart attacked the giant. After the ebb and flow of much fighting, Great-Heart beheaded the giant with his sword.

Christiana asked Great-Heart, "Are you wounded?"

"A small wound, proof of my love to my Master and a means by grace of increasing my final reward."

"Weren't you afraid?" asked Christiana.

"It is my duty to distrust my own ability, so I may rely on Him who is stronger than all."

"And what of you?" Christiana asked of the man Great-Heart had rescued.

"Even after the giant Slay-Good took me,"

said the man, "I thought I would live. For I heard that any pilgrim, if he keeps his heart pure toward the Lord, will not die by the hand of the enemy."

"Well said," agreed Great-Heart. "Who are you?"

"Feeble-Mind." He seemed reluctant to continue on the way with the others. "You are all lusty and strong. I will be a burden." Just then a man approached on crutches. "And what of him?"

"I am committed to comfort the feebleminded and to support the weak," said Great-Heart.

As they continued in the way, there came one running to meet them. He said, "Gentlemen, and you of the weaker sort, if you love life, shift for yourselves, for the robbers are before you."

They stayed alert, searching all the turnings where they could have met the villains. But they never came to the pilgrims.

About this time Christiana wished for an inn for herself and her children because they were very tired. Then Honest said, "There is one a little before us where a very honorable disciple, Gaius, lives."

So they all decided to turn in there because the old gentleman gave him so good a report. So when they came to the door, they went in. Then they called for the master of the house, and they asked if they might lie there that night.

"Yes," said Gaius, "if you speak truth. My house is for none but pilgrims."

So gladdened that the innkeeper loved pilgrims, they called for rooms. While the servants prepared a late supper, they had good conversation with the innkeeper.

The company and conversation were so good, the group stayed for a month at the inn, getting refreshment they needed after their various trials. While there, Matthew and Mercy were married, and Gaius gave his daughter Phebe to James as his wife.

Finally the day came to leave the inn. Gaius refused payment, saying that he received all he needed from the Good Samaritan. As they all went on, they neared Vanity. Knowing the trials Christian and Faithful faced in that town, they discussed how they should pass through the town. Finally Great-Heart said, "I have, as you know, often been a conductor of pilgrims through this town. I know of a man at whose house we may lodge. If you think good, we will turn in there."

They all agreed, and as they came to the town, evening fell. But Great-Heart knew the way and they were soon settled into the house with their host, Mnason.

Because of the fellowship they found in that

house, the group stayed there for a long time. Before they left, Mnason gave his daughter Grace to Samuel to wed, and his daughter Martha to Joseph. During the time they stayed in Vanity, the pilgrims came to know many of the good people of the town and did them what service they could.

While they were there, a monster came out of the woods and slew many of the people of the town. It carried away their children. No man in the town dared to face this monster. All the men fled when they heard the noise of his coming.

The monster had a body like a dragon with seven heads and ten horns. Now Great-Heart, together with those who came to visit the pilgrims at Mnason's house, made a covenant to destroy the beast. They went to battle against the monster so many times, they wore the beast down through multiple wounds, so that they expected the monster to die. This made Great-Heart and his companions greatly famed throughout the town.

Finally the time came for the pilgrims to resume their pilgrimage. So they prepared for their journey. They sent for their friend, conferred with them, and committed each other to the protection of their Prince. So they went forward on their way.

Soon they came to the place where Faithful

was put to death. They stopped and thanked Him who had enabled him to bear his cross so well. Thus they passed through the fair.

They passed the hill of Lucre where the silver mine claimed By-Ends and others. They passed the pillar of salt that had been Lot's wife. There they considered how intelligent men could be so blinded as to turn aside here. Only as they considered again that nature isn't affected with the harms men meet up with, then they could understand the attracting virtue upon the foolish eye.

They went on till they came to the river that was on this side of the Delectable Mountains. Here they committed their little ones to Him who was Lord of this meadow. Beyond the River of God they came to By-Path Meadow where the stile led to Doubting Castle. Great-Heart halted at the warning left by Christian. Here they discussed what was best to do.

"I have a commandment to 'fight the good fight of the faith.' And who is a greater enemy of faith than the giant Despair?" Suddenly Great-Heart led the others off the way and over the stile to find Doubting Castle. When they approached the castle, they knocked for entrance with an unusual noise.

Despair rushed out, yelling, "Who are you?" His wife, Diffidence, followed.

"Great-Heart, one of the King's protectors for pilgrims to the Celestial City. I demand of you that you open your gates for my entrance. Prepare yourself for battle, for I am come to take away your head and to demolish Doubting Castle."

"I have conquered angels," bragged Despair. So he put on his armor and went out to fight.

Yet Great-Heart assaulted him so savagely, Diffidence came out to help. Honest cut her down with one blow. Despair fought hard, with as many lives as a cat, but died when Great-Heart cut off his head. It took the pilgrims seven days to destroy the castle. Yet Great-Heart warned:

"Though Doubting Castle is demolished,
And the giant Despair has lost his head,
Sin can rebuild the castle, make it remain,
And make Despair the giant live again."

❧

They took the giant's head with them when they went back to join the rest of their group. They had a party to celebrate the end of the giant Despair, his wife Diffidence, and Doubting Castle. When they left the area, Great-Heart put the giant's head on a pillar that Christian erected to warn pilgrims who came after him. Then he wrote under the head on the marble,

This is the head of him, whose name only
In former times did pilgrims terrify.
His castle's down, and Diffidence his wife
Brave Master Great-Heart has bereft of life.
Despondency, his daughter Much-Afraid,
Great-Heart, for them also the Man has play'd.
Who hereof doubts, if he'll but cast his eye
Up hither, may his scruples satisfy.
This head also, when doubting cripples dance,
Doth show from fears they have deliverance.

Then the company moved forward along the way. When the pilgrims reached the Delectable Mountains, they were welcomed by the shepherds Knowledge, Experience, Watchful, and Sincere. The pilgrims feasted, then rested for the night. The next morning, with the mountains so high and the day clear, the shepherds showed them many things. On one mountain they saw Godly-Man, clothed in white, being pelted with dirt by two men, Prejudice and Ill-Will. The dirt would not stick to his clothes. On another mountain a man cut clothes for the poor from a roll of cloth, yet the roll of cloth never got smaller.

The pilgrims left singing. Along the way was a man with sword drawn and face bloody. "I am Valiant-for-Truth," he said. "I was set upon by three men: Wild-Head, Inconsiderate, and Pragmatic.

They gave me three choices: become one of them, go back on the way, or die. I fought them for hours. They fled when they heard you coming."

"Three to one?" marveled Great-Heart.

" 'Though an army besiege me, my heart will not fear,' " replied Valiant-for-Truth.

"Why did you not cry out?"

"Oh, I did—to my King."

Then said Great-Heart to Valiant-for-Truth, "You have behaved yourself worthily. Let me see your sword."

So Valiant-for-Truth showed him the blade. Great-Heart studied it for a while, then said, "Ha! It is a right Jerusalem blade."

Valiant-for-Truth said, "It is so. The man who holds it need not fear it. Its edges will never blunt. It will cut flesh and bones and soul and spirit and all."

"You have done well," Great-Heart said.

Then they took Valiant-for-Truth and washed his wounds and gave him of what they had to refresh him. And so he joined the company of pilgrims.

By the time they were better acquainted with Valiant-for-Truth, they now walked the Enchanted Ground, where the air made them drowsy. Then a great darkness fell over them, and they walked blindly. Thorns tore them, bushes tripped them, and they lost shoes in the mud. All about them was mud, purposely made to smother pilgrims. Yet with Great-Heart leading and Valiant-for-Truth bringing up the rear, they made their way.

They reached an arbor, warm and cozy. A soft couch was there for weary bones. Great-Heart warned them, however, that it was a temptation, a trap. At the next arbor they found two men, Careless and Too-Bold, fast asleep. They could not be awakened. The Enchanted Ground was very deadly because it was so near Beulah that pilgrims thought they were at last safe.

They came upon a man on his knees. Honest knew him. "He is Standfast, a right good pilgrim. What happened, Standfast?"

"A woman of great beauty came to me. She spoke soothingly and smiled at the end of every sentence. She offered me her body, her purse, and her bed. I am very lonely, I am very poor, and I am very weary, but I turned her down several times. And yet she persisted: If only I would let her rule me, she said, she would make me so happy. She said she is the mistress of the world, Madam Bubble. I fell to my knees as you see me now and prayed to Him above who could help me. She only just left me."

"She is a witch," said Great-Heart. "It is her sorcery that enchants this ground. Anyone who lays his head down on her lap lays it on the chopping block."

The pilgrims trembled, yet sang for joy:

"What danger is the pilgrim in?
How many are his foes?
How many ways there are to sin, no living
*   mortal knows.*
Some do escape the ditch, yet can fall
*   tumbling in the mire.*
Some though they shun the frying pan
*   do leap into the fire!"*

After this, they came into the land of Beulah, where the sun shines night and day. Here, because they were weary, they betook themselves awhile to rest. And because this country was common for pilgrims, and because the orchards and vineyards that were here belonged to the King of the Celestial City, they were licensed to make bold with any of His things. But a little while soon refreshed them here, for the bells did so ring and the trumpets continually sounded so melodiously that they could not sleep. And yet they received as much refreshing as if they had slept their sleep never so soundly.

One day a messenger came to Feeble-Mind. The Master wanted him to cross the river to the Celestial City. The entire company went with him to the river. His last words as he entered the river were, "Welcome, life."

Honest departed next. His last words were, "Hold out, faith and patience."

As he departed, Christiana said, " 'Here is a true Israelite, in whom there is nothing false.' I wish you a fair day and a dry river when you set out for the Celestial City, but as for me, come wet or dry, I long to go."

One by one over the weeks the pilgrims left. Valiant-for-Truth said, "Death, where is your sting?" as he entered the river, then, "Grave, where is your victory?" as he crossed over.

One day a messenger brought Christiana a letter:

> *Hail, good woman! I bring you tidings: the Master calls for you, and expects you to stand in His presence, clothed in Immortality, within ten days.*

༄

When the day came that Christiana must go, the road was full of people to see her take her journey. The banks beyond the river were full of horses and chariots, which had come down from above to accompany her to the City Gate.

So she came and entered the river with a beckon of farewell to those who followed her to the riverside.

As she entered the river, she said, "I come, Lord, to be with You, and bless You." Behind her, her children wept, but Great-Heart clashed the cymbals for joy.

It would be many, many years before the Lord called for Christiana's sons, who with their wives greatly increased the church in Beulah.